CASTING CONFESSIONS

EROTIC TALES

ANTHOLOGY

EDITED BY

DAVID

MACMILLAN

companion press

laguna hills, california
http://www.companionpress.com

How To Be A Pornstar © 1999 by Alan W. Mills
Garage Sale © 1999 by Barry Alexander
The Headmaster And The Rent Boys © 1999 by Tom MacDougal
Screen Test © 1999 by Ruthless
Crashers © 1999 by Alex Corey
Special Talent © 1999 by Dominic Santi
Nice Work If You Can Get It © 1999 by W.M. Williams
In Security © 1999 by David Logan
In Search Of … © 1999 by Vic Howell
Type Casting © 1999 by Michael Stamp
Cock Rock © 1999 by Murray Brown
Stairway To Stardom © 1999 by J.D. Ryan
Stunt Cock © 1999 by Bill Crimmin
The Life Saver © 1999 by George Dibbs
Dances With Coyote © 1999 by Bryan Nakai
Made Man © 1999 by Simon Sheppard
Passport To Porn © 1999 by David MacMillan

COMPANION PRESS, PO Box 2575, Laguna Hills, California 92654

Printed in the United States of America
First Printing 1999

ISBN: 1-889138-17-7

Library of Congress Catalog Card Number: 99-72643

Cover photo of Matt Bradshaw courtesy Per Lui

Contents

Introduction

No, THE WRITERS DIDN'T HAVE TO SLEEP WITH ME TO GET INTO THIS collection—but only because I didn't think of it until now!

How do so many handsome young men with such well-developed packages end up in the porn videos we watch? How do they get in? How are they selected?

Well, read the tales in this collection and you'll find out.

We've all heard stories about talent scouts and casting couches, but are the stories really true?

According to the writers in this collection they are. As I read one confession after another I had a difficult time knowing how much of what I was reading was fiction and how much was fact.

Who would have thought a hairy security guard could score such a smooth beauty as David Logan's stud did in "In Security"? Then I had the opportunity to meet the man on whom the character Shane was modeled. I tried not to drool.

What French director would go exploring Charleston, South Carolina as J.D. Ryan has Armand Bettencourt do? I was more than slightly surprised when I met J.D. and "Armand" recently (J.D. reminds me more than a bit of Johan Paulik and I now appreciate both "Armand's" talent as a director *and* his taste in men a lot more than I did).

And I did meet Jeb Stuart and Jan Tonkovic when I was in Prague last year. Truly lovely lads. They appear in "Passport To Porn." Jaroslav and another lad under exclusive contract to Jeb showed me around the capital of the Czech Republic.

It was quite difficult to choose which stories would go into this collection. There were so many confessions that found their way into my mailbox. I guess confession *is* good for the soul, not to mention the body. I hope these authors feel better—I know I do. And I think you will too.

Among my favorite stories are Barry Alexander's "Garage Sale," J.D. Ryan's "Stairway To Stardom," and Mick Stamp's "Type Casting."

One or two of the tales in this book may not be completely true, but it doesn't matter because they're all hot. Whatever your tastes, be prepared to read this book with one hand. It's that kind of anthology.

Do you have a casting couch fantasy or real-life confession of your own that you would like to share? If so, e-mail it to me at dtam01@aol.com. Maybe it'll make it into the next edition.

David MacMillan

Atlanta Geogia, 1999

How To Be A Pornstar

Alan W. Mills

STEP ONE: GET CONNECTED.

"So, why do you want to do porn?" Jeff asked, waiting for his ball to emerge from the machine to his left. The whole alley sounded like Kurt Cobain wailing on a mine field.

"I'm not saying I do," I kind of shouted. "I just want to know what I'd have to do if I did." I glanced over at Jeff's five pins. He was going for a spare, but he didn't have a chance. His pins were split into two groups—there was no way he could hit them both.

"You know," he said, "you don't have to do this."

"Do what?"

Jeff inserted three fingers into the holes of his red, marbleized ball. "Find common ground. I'm not hung up about what I do." He lifted the thing with a strong hand, the weight of it making his forearm defined.

Jeff walked to the mouth of the aisle, swung the ball up to his chin, supported it with his left hand, composed himself, released the weight, letting it carry his arm back then forward until the ball escaped his grasp, fell to the hardwood floor, and sailed down its long, narrow and predetermined path. The ball had an odd spin to it. It threatened the gutter but curled back, striking three of the pins at an angle and sending one of them flying at the other two.

I sat expressionless, not believing he had pulled it off. The rack lowered and a bar came down to sweep away the evidence. This kind of shit just doesn't happen, I thought. Someone has to be making this up. I looked down at the score I'd been keeping. "You win," I said.

Jeff sat next to me. "I know."

"You're not supposed to beat someone on a first date."

"Ever read Sacher-Masoch?" he asked.

"Yeah," I said, "*Venus In Furs.*"

"Then you know about the hammer and the anvil."

I smiled. "Is that what I should expect from you?"

He grinned broadly, looked over his shoulder, then looked back. "Certainly not on a first date," he said with a coy glint that made me feel all twisted inside.

STEP TWO: Arrange An Interview.

Back in my own shoes, I took the Miller Lite that Jeff offered. The alley's bar was crowded and the music, which had been bearable when competing with clashing balls and pins, was now incredibly loud. Every song in this place was harsh and disagreeable. It was all part of my generation's movement to haphazardly appropriate the dying past and give it a noisy and spit-shined spin. "So, tell me, how did you get into it?" I shouted.

"Are you still on that?" he shouted almost right into my ear. "Look, I don't want to talk about it."

"What do you want to talk about then?"

"I want to talk about you! You're so fucking beautiful!" he yelled, and like a reflex, my eyes scanned the straights that congregated around us. None of them even noticed, the music was so loud. Jeff grinned, somewhat laughing at me. "When I first saw you, I couldn't believe how intriguing you were! Your accent alone made my cock fucking rock hard!"

"I've been attracted to you for a long time!"

"I know that!" he yelled. "Right now, I just want to drop to my knees and suck your cock 'til you cum in my mouth! Do you think anyone would notice?!"

I laughed. A girl behind me laughed too, but that was to something someone else had shouted.

Jeff moved in close to me, his lips almost touching my ear. "Every time you went to throw your ball, I kept thinking about eating the fuck out of your ass. Goddammit, I just want to spread your ass apart really hard and lick deep into your soft, pink hole. Your hole is pink, isn't it? And your ass is smooth and milky. I bet you made sure you were good and clean before you came out here tonight, didn't you? You spent all day thinking about getting fucked, huh?" His fingers touched my wrist, and he guided my hand, the one that held the bottle, to his crotch. The back of my fingers touched it. "By this cock," he whispered, guiding my fingers up and down its massive, fat, solid length. The back of his hand pressed against my own hard cock.

"Yeah," he said, "you wanna get fucked so bad it hurts, don't you?" His fingers let go of my wrist, but I continued to rub his swollen cock and cum-heavy nuts with the back of my hand. "That's right," he whispered. I could barely hear him. "That cock belongs to you. And I'm gonna fuck you with it 'till you fall in love."

He pulled back quickly and grinned around the neck of his bottle as he sucked his beer down. I took a sip from mine, feeling sweaty and constricted, like someone had wrapped iron plating around my chest. I looked up at him and his beer had disappeared. He lowered the bottle again and set it on a nearby table. I put my bottle down too. He stepped behind me and steered me out with his hand firmly on my shoulder.

STEP THREE: Make An Impression.

I couldn't believe how big Jeff's house was. It was huge and filled with high-end furniture. It reminded me of my parents' home in Montreal. In the entry was a Planas, and I could see another one hanging in the main living room. "How much money do you make?" I blurted before considering how rude I might sound.

Jeff took my hand and led me into an office to our left. "This all belongs to a friend. He's in Prague right now, owns Top Dog Studios. He lets me stay here a lot."

"That's nice of him," I said as Jeff let go of my hand and walked behind his friend's French Provincial desk.

Jeff sat down in his friend's leather chair and said, "In this world, nothing ever really belongs to you. You just use what other men offer."

"Sounds familiar."

"Does it?" he said, changing his whole demeanor, even the tone of his voice. It was as if he'd gone from his late twenties to his mid-fifties in just a quick snap of the fingers. Pretending to be a director, he said, "So, Jeff tells me you're really hot and you want to be in one of my movies."

"Excuse me?" I gazed at Jeff who was still pretending to be someone else.

Jeff looked away, exasperated, and glared back at me. "You do want to do movies, don't you? I hope you and Jeff aren't wasting my time."

"No, sir," I said. "Um, yeah, I want to do movies. How does that all work?"

"Call me Charlie."

"Okay... Charlie."

"Good. Let's see your cock."

"W—What?"

"Your cock. Show me your cock."

I undid my Diesel's, feeling awkward and unsure of what was going on. "You aren't shy," he asked, "are you? Because if you are, you're gonna really hate it when a whole crew is watching you get fucked up the ass."

I pulled my dick out. It was soft and unimpressive. "Fucked? I thought—"

"No! Now look, if you're gonna do this, I'm gonna wanna use you as a bottom. You're too boyish to be a top and, besides, I'm casting a bottom for the picture I'm working on. So that's that. Maybe I can use you as a top later, but I have to see you get fucked first. Okay?"

I didn't know what to say.

"Um, can you get your cock hard for me, please."

I looked down at my dick.

Jeff started flipping through papers on the desk and waved a pen in the direction of my crotch.

"Go on," he said, not even looking up at me.

I was already kind of hard from the tension. I took my shaft in hand and stroked it a bit. Jeff looked up to watch me. In only moments, I was hard and sticking straight out.

"Come here," he said. I stepped closer to him. He wrapped a fist around my fat shaft and pumped it a bit, squeezing it, making a drop of precum seep from my slit. "Nice," he said. "Turn around."

I did as I was told and pulled my Diesel's and Versace's down, exposing my ass just inches from his face. "Yeah, nice ass," he said. "This is the kind of ass men want for their money." He touched his cheek to my milky flesh and breathed deeply. "Yeah, real nice."

Jeff stood up behind me and pushed me forward a bit. "Bend over the desk, kid. Charlie wants to get a good look at your hole."

STEP FOUR: Steal The Show.

Jeff was stripped down, stroking a hard cock while aiming his compact, digital cam in my direction. I was spread wide open, lying back against plush pillows, making my cock feel warm and tingly for an audience I couldn't picture. I strangled my shaft and shook my cock at Jeff's technology, fingers splayed across my scrotum. Jeff moved closer, onto the bed, his muscular thighs brushing against my toes.

I spread my legs a bit more, lifted my knees, thrust my pelvis forward, showing Jeff's camera the pink hole with which he had become infatuated. I brought my middle finger down to it. I played with the soft flesh. Jeff moved in close.

Teasing him, I brought my finger to my mouth and sucked on it, getting it wet and slick and ready for my ass. I couldn't taste my own musk. Jeff had licked the scent from my hole. I tasted more like him than like me. I touched my hole again with the finger and pushed up, inward—I was already open to it, ready for it. I moaned, closing my eyes as I opened myself to Jeff's probing camera.

Jeff lifted my calves and pushed my thighs back over my stomach. He lifted his camera from his face, still pointing it down at my ass, and spit really hard at my tender, pink asshole. My finger was deep inside me, and his spit felt cold against my warmth.

Jeff got really close with his camera. I could hear the focus re-setting itself. With a free hand, he put his own finger to my hole and pushed it. I was twice as open to him then, his finger and my finger swirling around each other in the hidden depths of my body. He fucked into me with his finger, driving my own so deep that the rest of my hand stretched my ass at the hatch.

With my left hand, I stroked my cock. It was sticky with drying precum, but the stuff seeping out made it slick again as my fist moved over the sensitive head.

STEP FIVE: Market Yourself.

"Oh, I like that," he said, looking down through his camera as I licked the belly of his cock, tasting the salty tip, twisting my neck until the whole monster slipped into my mouth. My lips followed the shaft and his girth pressed down on my tongue until the whole of him was like some alien buried in my throat. "Oh fuck," he moaned, "that looks so fuckin' hot." His camera zoomed in; I pulled off and went back down, trying to get more of him inside me. I did it again, gurgling as I stretched my throat, pushing myself forward until I could smell the sweat embedded in his pubes.

Slowly stroking myself, spit drooled from my mouth, coating his cock and dripping down my chest. He shook his cock in my mouth. "Yeah, get that shit good and wet!" He fucked the thing down my throat, and I opened to it, letting saliva pour from my mouth.

I closed my lips around the shaft and vacuum-packed his fat mushroom head. I drank my own spit from his cock. The fluid sank down my throat, choking me. My cock got harder, got wetter in my hand. As I gagged he held my head to his crotch, forcing my chin to rub against his nuts. He stank of building sweat, sweet with pheromones, deep, dizzying.

He let me go and I fought the compulsion to pull away. I stayed latched to his cock about halfway, sucking air through my nose, swallowing, trying to make the salty mixture of spit and precum drain past my esophagus.

My jaw was tired, but I wanted to suck his cock all night. I went past the pain and opened to his full girth and let him once again push the wet, steamy warmth behind my teeth, down past my tongue.

"Oh man!" he said, pulling his cock from my mouth with his fingers wrapped around his nuts. I licked at the air, trying to get more. My cock burned with need, precum flooding out of the slit like I had a bottomless well.

"You're so fuckin' hot," he said, hitting his cock against my tongue before totally taking it away.

His camera panned up from my fist on my cock, to my tight stomach and heaving chest, to my pleading eyes and pouting, saliva-coated lips.

"I'm so fuckin' close," I said, staring straight through his lens. "Oh please, Charlie, I wanna cum with you fucking my mouth."

Jeff laughed behind his camera. He rubbed his cock against my mouth. "And then lick your cum off my feet?"

"Anything."

Precum drooled from his slit and stuck to my lips, trailing like a spider's web when he took a step back. "Oh no," he said, "I'm not done with you yet."

STEP SIX: Build A Fan Base.

His image flickered on a tiny screen inside the eyepiece. He had his fist wrapped around my shaft, a gray line flying from top to bottom as his head moved up and down. I viewed, in awe, as my cock disappeared behind his nose, his eyes hidden by short pale bangs that almost touched my pubes. I thrust up into his mouth, my movement looking like a detached act, small and far away. It was jagged, my cock one place and then suddenly another.

I felt it though, the feeling real, making my toes curl, making my legs tense up and tense up more as Jeff worked my cock with firm lips. He cupped my nuts in powerful hands and touched my asshole with inconsistent fingers. He grabbed behind my knees and lifted the lower part until my ass was open to him. He had one knee on the black leather sofa, one foot on the floor. My neck kinked up as he pushed me harder against the armrest, my sweaty back sticking to the cushion. I had to hold the camera with both hands to keep it steady while Jeff went for my ass.

"Oh fuck!" I groaned. I could feel his tongue lap at my hole; it looked like it was happening to someone else. He pressed down on my thighs. I felt the tension. My feet dangled in the air, my toes almost undefined on the tiny, dull screen.

Jeff licked up my ass to my clenched-up nads. My cock pointed straight down at me. I could almost make out moisture on the tip. It was primeval, reminding me of caves. Stalactites holding tight to the ceiling, my cock dripping mineral-rich water. Stalagmites thinking they might reach the roof, my tongue stretching to taste the upper world.

Looking up from licking my nuts, Jeff smiled, saliva dripping down his chin. "Dude, you got a hot ass! You fuckin' taste good!" He pulled my cock up to his mouth like a lever and sucked it in, letting it pop out all wet and slimy. It made a smacking sound against my abs.

He lowered my ass back to the sofa and moved up my body. His lips kissed my pelvis and the joint of my leg. He licked at my stomach and navel, and kissed my ribs. As he bit into my nipple, his hair went blurry. I couldn't make him out then. He blocked the light like a dragon eating the sun, and I could feel his teeth in my skin, around the areola. He looked like a cloud and like darkness, and his hand brushed the camera aside, sending the hand that held it to the floor. He kissed me deeply, his wet lips soaking me in our mixed fluids.

I let go of the camera and held him, his whole heavy body pressing down on me. I felt like Atlas, and Jeff's dense muscles were like mountains and valleys borne aloft by my skin, his mouth like an ocean dripping spit onto my tongue. I thought about the camera, imagining the something else it saw, the way the audience would interpret the upturned image of a vacant room.

STEP SEVEN: Pace Yourself.

I was bent over a red, padded bench. Mirrors lined the room. Jeff's cock slid into my ass with little effort. I was open and ready for him, my flank raising in anticipation of his descent. I gripped the rack in front of me and held on.

Jeff pulled out and thrust back in. "Shit!" he exclaimed. "This is so fucking hot. You should see this!"

I felt him lifting me on his cock. It was buried all the way and he raised himself from his knees slowly, creating pressure beneath my spine. He forced me up with him, and I put one knee on the bench, the other half-bent, my toes vainly digging into the rubber mat floor. I balanced my weight on the rack. One hand slapped the mirror—the one I watched my eyes in—and left a steamy print.

Jeff had even better access to the secret me. He guided my second knee to the bench and just went off. I looked to my right. Jeff was in the mirror, mounting me like a dog. He was driving his hips forward, his large and infamous cock disappearing into some hidden recess I couldn't see. But he could see it. He had the camera pointed at it, and through technology, he recorded the connection I felt deep inside. And then not so deep. And then.

Suddenly. All the way in. "Oh, fuckin' damn. I can't believe how cool this is," he said, grinning sideways in the mirror. I clenched my ass and rode his cock with fury. I threw my head back, gave him true vengeance, and gripped his cock with parts of me I've never seen. He held on to my ass with his left hand, still filming, but I knew when I looked at the mirror that his eyes were closed and raised to the ceiling, his mouth agape, his digital video camera clenched to his chest, still pointed down.

He took deep breaths and stopped his thrusting. He held himself inside and looked back into his device. I pumped myself slowly on him and watched his lens trace up my spine, to my face. I continued guiding my ass onto and off of him, closing my eyes, knowing it was watching. "Yeah, bitch," he groaned, "work that fuckin' cock. Yeah, you bitch, you love that fuckin' cock, bitch, you love that fuckin' cock."

I felt him squeeze the shaft like it was a bottle he needed to empty. His thumb and forefinger pushed against my hole. "Oh, man, keep fuckin' me with your cock. I love that shit, Charlie, I fuckin' love it."

I opened my eyes and watched his camera follow my glance to the mirror that framed us. "Yeah," he moaned, "you're one greedy little pig-bitch." I could hear his breathing, smell the fresh sweat clinging to our bodies. "Oh fuck!" he grunted. "Yeah—you're gonna fuckin' get it now!"

STEP EIGHT: Make Investments.

Jeff looked like a tiny, dull-colored God inside the camera. He held my calves against his chest and pounded his cock as hard into my ass as he could. He was grunting like an ape, like a big jock beating up a freshman.

His blond hair was dark with sweat. Bitter, salty fluids dripped down his face. I wanted to look at him with real eyes just to make sure his image wasn't faked.

Me, I had trouble breathing and clung to the camera like it was a pillow. I needed to sink my teeth into it. I felt nothing but cock, pounding in, pulling out, thundering deep deep inside me, smashing into every part, shattering me like the mirrors that stood around us.

I had trouble keeping my eyes open. My hard cock smacked against my stomach with every thrust. I couldn't stop the slapping. Without both hands on Jeff's camera, I'd lose control.

Through the camera, Jeff's face looked twisted. I zoomed in on the pain, the torture in his eyes.

He was holding back as hard as he could, holding back like a professional, giving me every second he could spare. I watched his eyes clench shut, his lips curl and bare his teeth, which were separated just enough to let his high pitched cry escape.

I zoomed back and caught his cock coming out, saw the condom go flying past my thigh, recorded the first evidence of cum, the first flow snaking out, the massive volley splattering the air, the single powerful shot followed by another and then a smaller one, and then the final downpour, the smaller drops, the last remnants getting squeezed from his slit and wiped away with his thumb.

Jeff rubbed his sticky hands on my legs and took the camera from my grip. I smiled, looking at all the cum scattered atop my skin. I fisted my cock for him, for the audience back home, and stroked it, letting his cum make it glossy and slick. I grabbed my nuts, showing my worked-over ass to the camera. And I came. I came with a force that betrayed excitement. I came like a fountain, shooting spunk high into the air.

When I stopped breathing so heavily and opened my eyes, Jeff lowered the camera and shut it off. My cum-covered chest still heaved a little, and Jeff kneeled down on the mat next to me, looking straight into my eyes.

I watched him scan my torso and my sloppy, waning cock. He was smiling, and he kissed me. I tasted sweetness, but it wasn't like the real kind. It was something in my head, something in the way his lips cupped mine and held themselves there, tightening, holding, and letting go.

The semen began to cool and I felt afraid to move. Cum already started dripping down my sides. I began to laugh, and Jeff laughed too. "Oh man," he said, "I could make you famous."

STEP NINE: Know That Nothing Lasts Forever.

The chimes of the front door woke me. I grabbed my robe and half-assed my way downstairs, rubbing my eyes through each blind step. I opened the door while still standing behind it, and my boyfriend stepped in. "Oh," he said, "you just woke up."

"Aren't you brilliant today."

"Where were you last night?" He followed me through the living room to the kitchen, where I planned on making coffee. "I called you, but you weren't home." I stared at him. He gave me a kiss.

"Sorry," he said. "Good morning."

"Good morning to you too." I gave him my first smile of the day.

As I filled a filter with my favorite, Kenyan, I spied the digital cassette hiding underneath my keys.

Feeling guilty, I turned around. My boyfriend sat. His eyes studied me. "Do you still want to rollorblade today?"

I scratched my scalp with all my fingers and tried to tame my hair. "Not really," I said.

"What are you in the mood for?" he asked, shaking dark bangs from his eyes with a twitch of his head.

"Oh, rollorblading's fine." I pulled out a chair and sat next to him. He was still curious, and I knew he knew that something had happened. I gave him a kiss—a quick, boyfriend kind of one—and felt like I should salvage this. I grinned mischievously, thinking of a way to compromise. "How 'bout we stay in and make a porno."

"What?"

"We could even sell it or something?" I watched his eyes.

"You're kidding, right?" He huffed. "You don't really want to be in porn, do you?"

"No, not really," I said, feeling kind of torn, feeling like exposing myself last night was a more honest thing. "I just thought something different would be fun."

"Well, don't," he said, like he was Nancy Reagan. "Something like that could change your life forever."

I laughed. My boyfriend didn't know it, but that was exactly what Jeff had said.

"What's so funny?" he asked.

"Nothing," I said, getting up to start the coffee.

Garage Sale

Barry Alexander

YOU EVER WONDER WHY THEY ALWAYS HAVE SUCH BUTT-UGLY couches in porn vids?

It's not that directors don't appreciate style, but a couch is much more than just a scene prop. It has to have strength, durability, a certain screen presence all its own. It has to stand out and say Hey! Look at me! This is where all the action is happening.

Sure a French Provincial in moiré silk looks classy, and overstuffed crushed velvet traditionals give a homey touch, but they're not durable. You get a 200 pound muscle-hunk fucking the shit out of someone on one of those and you have kindling.

A good vid couch has to be stain resistant as well. Sweat, cum, beer, drool—the casting couch sees them all. And some stars really don't like to get fucked with their faces down in the mingled body odors of the last hundred guys. Go figure.

I'd never minded when I was acting in vids. It always made me horny wondering about the last guys who had fucked on the couch. If the guy I was with wasn't doing it for me, I could fantasize about all the hot men who had been here before me. Once you're the director, you have to consider every actor's preferences. There's no arguing with a hard dick.

So, anyway, when Dick Spears and Rod Cruise broke the couch during the filming of *All The Right Places*, I knew I was in trouble. I couldn't just go to a furniture store and buy a replacement. They don't make them that way anymore. Quality construction went out in the '60s.

I still hadn't decided what I was going to do as I drove back from lunch. Sure, I could improvise on this vid. A fuck over the desk is always good, and viewers love the stand-and-deliver. But stars complain about 2 hours flat on their backs on a desk and you can't move every story into the bedroom. Sometimes the plot just demands a couch.

I found myself stuck in a single lane of traffic crawling past road construction vehicles. Damn! It just wasn't my day. The street department *would* pick today to finally fill the potholes. When I spotted a gap between a dump truck and a barricade, I squeezed through onto a side street. I smirked at the fools still waiting patiently in line as I drove down the near empty street. I made a couple left turns that I thought would get me back in the right direction, but I soon found myself tangled in a maze of suburban streets.

The damned streets back there were jammed with badly parked cars. Where in the hell was the main road? And why in the hell did everyone have to have a garage sale? I swerved to miss a woman who trotted between the cars, clutching a butt-ugly lamp I wouldn't have put in my dog's house.

I finally decided to stop for directions the third time I passed the same puke green house. I shot into an empty parking spot a station wagon was considering. I was out of my car and walking up the driveway while the woman was still swearing. You snooze, you lose.

A cute young guy sat behind a card table with his feet propped on top of a cash box. A half-empty bag of salt-free, fat-free, taste-free bagel chips and a bottle of designer water sat beside him. I couldn't tell if the guy was asleep or just ignoring me. I studied my reflection in his mirrored sunglasses as I waited for him to say something.

I still had the face, even if the body had gone a little soft around the middle—well, maybe more than a little. And I always *had* spent more time at the gym cruising than I did on the Nautilus equipment. Somehow the gain didn't seem worth the pain anymore. But I had occasional regrets about losing the body I'd had in my twenties. I had even gone out and bought an ab-roller my last birthday. It'd been a month and I didn't see a difference. Still, soft or not, I had the face, so maybe the guy *was* asleep.

This guy was very cute. He had one of those endearing attempts at a mustache that young guys have, the kind that softly tickles as it brushes against your lips and nipples. His dark brown hair was thick and shiny and held back in a short ponytail. I felt an urge to remove the band and let his hair spill over my hand to see if it was really as silky as it looked. He wore one of those fishnet tank tops. I could see the dark coins of his nipples with the tiny peak at the center. I pictured someone teasing them with a wet tongue until they were hard and the swollen points poked out between the mesh of his shirt.

I followed the line of his long legs all the way up inside his baggy shorts. If I bent over slightly, I would have had the full view. I wondered if he wore underwear. I could see the sharp definition of his abs. My stomach used to look like that. Maybe I would take the damned ab-roller out of the box when I got home.

Well, I wasn't here to ogle the locals or play out porn scenarios in my head. Although this one would be fun. I could just see Rod Cruise bending down to check out this guy's goodies and getting caught. "Something there you'd like to see?" he'd ask in a mock gruff voice. He'd shift his legs so the camera would move in for a close-up of his furry low-hangers, visible though his shorts. Then Rod would slowly slide his hand up the guy's leg and...

I did tend to get lost in my work.

I cleared my throat. Sleeping Beauty didn't move. I wished I hadn't thought of that particular name. I started thinking about all the places I'd like to kiss him to wake him up. My cock squirmed and started to fill. Damn. Occupational hazard. "Excuse me."

He jumped. "Oh, hi. Sorry, I must have dozed off. Find something you like?"

Yeah, but he didn't have a price tag hanging off it. I cast a glance around the garage so I wouldn't be tempted just to stare at his crotch. Now I knew why I'd found a parking place in front of his house. I'd never seen such ugly furniture in my life. Just as I was about to make a smart-ass remark, I saw it.

The couch.

MY couch.

Square and sturdy. A solid couch that could stand up to assaults by muscle-bound body builders. Naugahyde can take multiple fluids and come back for more. And blue. Electric blue. A color that would draw every eye right to it and that would show off the glorious tans of Hot Stuff models.

I had to have it.

We'd finally come to an agreement when a young guy came storming into the garage. He was cute, too, in a punk kind of way. His short-cropped hair was so blond it was almost white. A row of earring studs in rainbow colors sparkled along his left lobe. His features were delicate, almost elfin, but his body was very muscular. He wore a sleeveless fuchsia-colored shirt that showed off his golden tan. Above the deeply scooped neck, a sprinkling of chest hairs shone gold in the sunlight. His eyes were as blue as the water in a chlorinated pool and right now they were narrowed in anger.

"What the fuck do you think you are doing, Shane? That's my stuff. I told you I was coming back for it."

"You got the last two month's rent?" Shane stood up and moved out behind the table. The other guy had to look up to him, but he didn't seem the least bit intimidated.

"Rent! We were lovers!"

"That was before I found out where you were all those nights these last couple months."

"Uh, look, guys—this is interesting, but you've got my check. You can't back out now. I'll be back later. My couch better still be here."

"It will be," Shane said grimly. "We made a deal. I always keep my promises—unlike some people I could name."

"Yeah? Well, you—"

I headed back to my car. I had better things to do with my afternoon than listen to two queens scream at each other. Even if they were cute.

By the time I rounded up a truck and found my way back to 1269 Maidenflower Lane, it was after five. Most of the garage sales had shut down. I pulled into the drive. The garage door was shut, so I walked up to the house and rang the bell. I rang it again. And again.

Damn! The bastard wasn't home. Well, I'd paid for the damn couch; I wasn't leaving without it. I walked over and tried the garage door, but it was locked. So I walked around back to see if there was a side door that might be open.

There was. The knob turned. I smiled. My luck was starting to change. I opened the door and walked in. My couch was still there. And I was right about the color. It showed off to perfection the tans of the two naked guys fucking on it.

"Uh, excuse me, but I believe that's my couch."

Shane looked over his shoulder at me and grinned. He never missed a stroke as he kept pumping into the smooth white butt of the guy beneath him. "Hope you don't mind. Jesse and I will be through in a minute. Then it's all yours."

"No—uh—take your time."

I had nothing better to do, so I swung around the lawn chair he'd been sitting on earlier and sat down to watch. They were hot.

Jesse was sitting on the couch, hips rolled up and arms locked around his knees, pulling his legs wide open. A blissful smile played over his lips as Shane pounded his ass. He opened his eyes and winked at me as he wiggled his butt in appreciation. I could see the thick cylinder pushing into him, but I had no idea how long it was until Shane eased it out. And out. And out. Jesse must have had a well-trained ass to take one that big. But I could see from the way his hard dick waggled between them that he was enjoying every inch.

Shane pulled it all the way out. I leaned closer to get a better look. The fucker had to be at least nine inches long. The translucent condom glistened with lube. Jesse wiggled his butt trying to make contact but Shane tipped his rod up and stoked it instead.

"Come on, Shane," Jesse protested.

"You want something?" Shane dropped his cock so it thumped against the blond's wide open hole with a wet smack. He slid it up and down the sweaty crevice. Jesse moaned every time it slid past his hungry hole.

"I want it. I want that big dick."

Shane pulled back and positioned his cock, but he didn't push it in. He teased Jesse, tickling his dilated anus with the rubber nipple at the end of the condom. He had great control, using only his hips to make subtle circles around his target.

Shane's hands were busy. Jesse had a tiny silver dagger through one nipple. Shane was busy tugging and twisting it while his mouth was making obscene sucking noises on the other nipple.

Jesse moaned and tossed his head as Shane bit down. Finally, he released the nipple with an audible pop. He had sucked it into a swollen, dark pink nub, glistening with saliva. Shane removed the dagger from the other nipple and plunged the tiny point through the one he had just molested. I gasped, expecting to see blood coursing down Jesse's chest, but from his reaction of pleasure, I quickly realized that both nipples must have been pierced.

"You've got such a hot ass. I'm going to shove this cock into it so hard you think you're getting fucked by Rod Cruise."

"Fuck me, Shane. Oh, God, just fuck me."

In one quick move, Shane impaled Jesse, pushing his cock so deep I couldn't even see his pubes. Jesse practically purred with contentment, his face totally blissed out. "Oh, yeah, give me every inch of that throbbing manmeat, baby."

I almost groaned at the godawful dialogue, but I soon forgot to be critical as I watched. They must have liked being watched; they were certainly putting on quite a show for me. It was as hot as anything I'd seen on a vid. I wished I'd brought a camera. The late afternoon sun shone through a dusty window and played over their sweat-glistened bodies. Their tans were a perfect complement to each other. One light gold and the other a rich chestnut. They looked wonderful against the bright blue Naugahyde. They were certainly photogenic. I wondered how good they were at taking directions.

"Pull out," I told Shane. "I want to see you fucking him doggy style."

He pulled out and Jesse flipped over, lying across the end of the couch so Shane could stand and fuck him. They moved as smoothly together as the most experienced stars. Neither hesitated. And neither softened as they took their new positions. Their cocks stayed rock hard. Shane buried his cock back inside Jesse's cute little bubble butt. His balls swung, smacking against Jesse with every stroke. He pounded into his lover like a fucking jackhammer. Jesse just begged him for more.

The cock threatening to pop the buttons of my 501's reminded me that I was not directing this particular scene. I didn't have to worry about camera angles and lighting. I could just enjoy. And I certainly was enjoying. I don't know if it was the wet, sloppy sounds of a good fuck or the intriguing potpourri of sweat and sex and Valvoline, but it was certainly working for me.

My cock demanded release. I stood up to free myself. I was so hard that I had a hard time unbuttoning. Ribbed white cotton welled into the opening as I released the final button. The head of my dick had pushed its way past the elastic waistband. I threaded the thick rod through my fly and let if poke out—ten inches of hard, veiny cock.

I heard a little gasp and smiled. Seems I wasn't the only one who was into watching. Jesse was staring wide-eyed at my personal assets. And Shane craned his neck around to get a look, too. Well, I did have a big one. That always helped when you did vids. I liked to think I had brought something more to the pictures I starred in, but I couldn't deny that it was the size of my dick that got me my first part, and the size of my expanding waistline that had cost me my last part. I didn't mind, not really. I had almost as much sex as a director as I'd had as a star, and all the chocolate I wanted to eat. It was well worth the trade off, and I still looked damned good.

I couldn't resist showing off a bit. Holding my jeans up so I wouldn't trip, I walked closer to give them the full picture. I fished out my balls too and let them hang. They were nice and furry now that I didn't shave them anymore. I spit into my hand and slopped saliva all over my bright red knob. They watched intently as I gently squeezed my cock, making the helmet even more prominent. Precome beaded in the opening and lengthened into a glistening thread. I caught it with the tip of my finger and dangled it over my mouth like a strand of spaghetti. I could be such a slut sometimes. I couldn't help grinning. Their eyes never left me. Shane's hips slowed to an easy in and out.

So I decided to give them a real show. I slipped out of my jeans and briefs, but left my white shirt on. The shirttail hung over my genitals, brushing against them as I moved, sending erotic tingles up my spine. I unbuttoned the middle buttons of my shirt and slipped my hand inside. I tugged and pinched my nipples, sending electric shocks straight to my cock and making it jump. When my nipples were hard, I walked over to the table and picked up the squeeze bottle of Evian. Standing in front of the couch, I squeezed the lukewarm water over the front of my shirt, soaking it and making it transparent. The warm water quickly cooled, tightening my nipples even more and making them push against the damp fabric.

I had their attention. Shane stopped pumping and held himself in place to watch me. Jesse encouraged me with catcalls and obscene remarks as I teased the hard nubs with my fingertips, sending delicious waves of sensation through my body. I peeled the wet shirt off so they could see my chest.

Water beaded on the dark line of hair running down my sternum. I squeezed more water between my nipples and let it slide over my abs. It trickled over my navel and flowed into the thicket of dark hair about my cock. The water followed the line of my shaft and dripped off the tip, like a miniature waterfall.

"Why don't you join us?"

I must have looked a bit surprised at Shane's question. I'd have expected it from Jesse, but Shane was the one who had complained about his lover sleeping around.

Shane grinned. "We've come to an understanding. We both play around as much as we want. But we always come home to each other."

"Sounds like a sensible arrangement to me."

My dick led the way as I walked over to join them. I considered my options for a moment. Shane's delectable ass was free, nicely muscled and solid-looking. I could see his dark hole winking at me as his hips returned to their endless drive. But there was something about the expression on Jesse's face—the utter abandon as he gave himself to pleasure. He grinned then and stuck his tongue out at me. I stared with fascination at the tiny silver ball piercing the tip.

Shane spread his legs a bit. It was tempting, but I resisted the invitation and settled for running my hands over the hard globes. I swatted him on the butt. "Maybe next time."

I sat down and pulled Jesse's head into my lap. His tongue glided out and slurped across my cock head. I pushed my hips forward. I shivered as the piercing slipped between my slit and moved up. God,

I had never felt anything so wonderful. I raked my fingers through the soft blond brush of his hair, holding him closer to me. He didn't really need any encouragement. The sensation from that shiny silver ball was almost unbearable. It probed the tiny opening, stroking the sensitive inner lips in a way I hadn't known was possible.

He opened wide and swallowed my cock. I didn't think I was ever going to get to the bottom of his throat. Then my pubes tangled with his mustache and I could go no deeper. I felt him swallow a couple of times. He seemed to have no problem breathing, so I just let my cock soak in the warmth of his throat for a while. I pulled back, dragging myself across his hot tongue. He curled the tip up, giving little licks to the underside as I withdrew. I gave him a moment to breath, then plunged back down his throat.

Shane held his hips in place while he continued his rhythmic assault. He must have really been doing a number on Jesse's prostate. Jesse whimpered with every thrust. He was trying to say something, but his mouth was too full for anything intelligible to come out. I didn't care. I loved the way his tongue fluttered around my cock and the little gulps he made as he tried to speak

I reached under him and explored his genitals. His cock wasn't huge, but I'll take a hard six-incher to a limp horsedick, any day. Jesse's cock was rock hard and drooling copious amounts of pre-come. His smooth balls rode his shaft. He was close.

I decided it would be safer to take my cock out his mouth for the moment. I sure as hell didn't want him biting down as he came. But God, it was hard to push that warm, sucking mouth away from my meat. "Just lick," I told him.

He got the message. The warm, wet tongue and the hard little ball piercing it felt wonderful on my nuts. He slurped and lapped eagerly. I closed my fingers around his rod. He moaned appreciatively and thrust his cock into my fist.

"Oh, God, Shane I'm coming!" Jesse cried. "I'm coming." He stiffened, his neck arching up as he came. Warm jizz flowed over my fist and I worked it gently over his shaft.

Shane was inspired to new efforts. He fucked Jesse so hard I swear he would have fucked him right off the couch if I hadn't been holding him in place. Shane flung his hair back with a toss of his head. His eyes were filled with lust.

"Oh, shit, baby, fill me with your hot load," Jesse encouraged him. Shane slammed his hips against Jesse's ass, trying to shove every last bit of his cock deep inside. His body quivered as he shot his load. "Oh fuck, I'm coming inside your hot tight ass."

Shane's breath came in sharp gasps as he collapsed against Jesse's back. I pushed Jesse's head back down to my balls and leaned forward to cover Shane's mouth with mine. Our tongues danced together as we tasted each other. His mustache brushed erotically across my upper lip as he sucked on my tongue.

My cock was throbbing as it searched for release. Jesse's tongue flicked all over my balls and left wet trails along the inside of my thighs. He lipped the underside of my cock, sucking gently. It felt wonderful but I wanted more.

"You got any more rubbers?" I asked. "Damn it, you two can't leave me like this."

Shane pulled out of Jesse and snapped off the condom. He tied it into a tight little package and made a perfect shot into the trash barrel. His cock was still half hard, drooping a bit to the left as it arched over his balls. It smacked against his thigh as he walked around the couch. He searched through the jumbled pile of their clothes, then held up a foil packet.

"Where do you want it?" he asked.

I couldn't answer for a moment I was staring eye to eye with his gorgeous cock. Thick blue veins scrolled along the still bloated shaft. The head was a bit smaller than the shaft and had a slight upward tilt. Great, a distinctive cock, one with personality, one with—skin! I smiled to myself as I noticed the skin slipping up to cover the rim of his cock. This was my lucky day.

Then Jesse did something amazing with that hot tongue of his and the only cock on my mind was the one throbbing between my legs. As randy as both guys were, I didn't think it would take either long to recover, but I wasn't willing to wait. I wanted some relief right then.

"Put it on me," I growled. "And get that mouth down here."

In two seconds, Shane was down on his knees in front of the

couch, rolling the safety over my aching prick. Then he gave Jesse one of the hottest open-mouthed kisses I had ever seen. I was starting to get pissed and even more horny when the two broke apart.

"I think we're neglecting our guest," Shane said as he gently brushed his lips across Jesse's one more time.

Jesse took the hint. He moved around to give Shane room and the two of them went to work. Shane swallowed my cock in one gulp. It coasted over his tongue and went right down. He held it there for a second, his lips mashed against my pubes, then started a vigorous sucking that really made me appreciate his talented mouth. Jesse kissed and slurped all over my scrotum then sucked one ball into his mouth. Both of them ran their hands all over my chest and thighs.

Then Shane worked a finger inside me. He found my prostate and gently bumped it. I almost came right then.

It was fantastic. Two hot men working on me with lips and hands and tongues. I knew I wasn't going to be able to hold out long with that kind of devoted attention, but I didn't care. I was too eager to come. A hot mouth on my cock, another worshiping my balls, a thick finger exploring and teasing my guts—I was in heaven.

Jesse paired his finger with Shane's and slid it inside me. The double thickness stretched me open. Their fingers squirmed inside me, bumping my prostate over and over again. My balls clamped against my cock, and Jesse had to settle for licking them, which he did with great enthusiasm.

Shane concentrated on the head of my dick, sucking gently and slurping over the glans. His tongue flicked at the little bundle of nerves under the crown. My legs started quivering as hot sparks shot up my spine.

"Oh shit! Oh fuck! God, I'm coming."

Shane's mouth plunged back down on my cock as the first spurts bubbled out of me. I splattered the inside of that condom, hosing it down with the biggest load I'd shot in weeks. I leaned against the couch, gasping for breath.

"You guys were fan-damn-tastic!" I finally managed to say.

"Think we could make it in one of your vids?" Shane looked up at me from between my legs with this totally innocent and conniving grin.

"How in the hell—"

"I recognized your name on the check, Barry."

I knew then I'd been set up. They had been trying to impress me.

I drove back to the studio with my couch in the back of the pickup. It had passed every test. Eye-catching, sturdy, waterproof. Everything I had wanted. I dropped it off at the studio so it would be ready for tomorrow's shoot.

I drove home. I was tired and hungry, but I still had some serious work to do.

People think directing vids is some kind of fantasy job. But it takes hard work and dedication. And a willingness to give up little things like sleep when there is a job to do. It also takes the ability to recognize a good thing when it's right under you—or over you.

I had two rookies showing up in the morning. I was damned if they were going to spout that awful dialogue in one of my films, though. They'd get it right if we had to practice all night.

The Headmaster And The Rent Boys

Tom MacDougal

"PUT IT IN HIM," MAX SAID AND PATTED MY BARE ARSE WITH HIS BIG hand; he was more rubbing it than patting it.

Iain groaned as my latex-covered prick spread his sphincter. "Slow now, Tim. Please," he whimpered and I began to believe that he really was a virgin.

"Give him time to get used to you being in his arse, lad," Max Molloy said from behind me. "Kiss him and twist his nipples a bit. I want to see you both look like you want this—" I looked back at him and he grinned. "I think you both would be good in this film, but there's got to be good chemistry between you."

I looked down at my connection with Iain. I was half-way into his hole, his cock had shriveled and was trying to hide under his foreskin. But his legs were gamely splayed for my entry. His eyes were closed tight in concentration and his soft, thin ginger hair fell back from his face and puddled on the cushion beneath us.

"Grind that bum around on his dick, lad," Max told him as I reached for both of his nipples.

I had been nervous as bloody hell as I waited. The chipped paint in the waiting room of the warehouse suite hadn't helped. Neither had the two lads sitting at the other end, even more nervous than I. At least they looked like they belonged in this south London neighborhood—dirty jeans, thin T-shirts, and nameless trainers, standard summer wear for this part of London. Me—I was dressed as what I was, a senior student at Kings College and the son of a successful barrister in Manchester.

I also accepted that I was gay, especially after Iain had ploughed my bum so thoroughly and so regularly. Before he told me he wasn't gay and went off to Scotland for the summer holiday, that is. But that was nearly a year ago. Iain was the last lad who'd found his way through my back door. The only one, too. I was at Global Entertainment because I had convinced myself that frolicking around naked would prove I was over him.

The two lads in the waiting room with me were definitely deep in denial; yet, they were here same as me. They acted as if they didn't know each other, and I reckoned they'd each done things for a few quid; but neither of them were happy that the other had to be guessing about those things now.

The advert in *Gay Outloud* magazine last week was explicit—Earn £500 for 10 hours of fun work. Six lads, versatile, with nice bodies. Career opportunity for the right person. Interviews on 15 May between 1PM and 7PM. The company was Global Entertainment and the advert had given this address. It was five after one, and the inner door was still closed.

I stood and started to cross to the grimey window to look out at what I could see of Eltham. The door opened behind me and I turned in time to see a man step into the room. His gaze went to the two lads immediately. "You sods are here? Didn't think you lads knew each other." Both went the color of beetroot. The man chuckled. "So, you didn't know about each other then? It might make for a cozy arrangement, don't you think?" They both seemed to try to sink into their chair cushions.

Whilst I was watching the local punks learn that the other was pink macho, I was taking in the man as well. He was a big sod, standing at least six-and-a-half feet and probably weighing eighteen stone. It all looked muscular. I got even more nervous.

"Let's see what you two can do together," the man told them. One of the boys pointed in my direction, and the man turned to me. "Sorry I didn't see you before. I'm Max Molloy and I'm casting several gay porno films. Are you in the right place?" I gulped, turned white, and nodded. "Okay then. Let me sort these two rentboys out and then we'll see about you." I nodded and he turned back to the lads from Eltham. "Let's go, guys," he said to them like a stern headmaster confronted with unruly Fourth Formers. "I want you naked fast—like one of your quickies in the alleyway."

I got back to a chair and collapsed in it. I started trying to convince myself to get up and leave. I was sure I wanted no part of this.

Iain's whole body jerked as I pulled at both nipples hard, his eyes opening wide. Max's hand on my arse shoved me into him. My pubes pressed hard against the insides of his thighs. He groaned. Slowly, he reached out and touched my smooth chest, spreading his long, bony fingers across most of it; he studied his hand touching me for a moment before his gaze moved up to my face.

I had forgotten how intensely blue his eyes were. How they would hold mine for hours at a time when I still thought he loved me. Before he'd left me. His lips formed into a tight little smile. "Shag me arse, Tim," he whispered. "Make it yours."

Max was on the floor between my legs, studying our union closely. "You two fit together nicely. Start to fuck him slow now."

The silence in the room was deafening. For about three minutes. "Christ, Max!" I heard from the office. "I can't take something as big as that," the voice bleated. There was a cry then and the same voice pleaded: "At least grease it up, mate. I ain't had nothing as big as that since the last time you did me."

I stared at the wall across from me. They were having sex in there. Two of them, if not all three. I didn't know what I'd been thinking when I decided to take the tube to Eltham. I just knew I wasn't ready to start having sex again—not like this. It'd been a bloody year! I'd be bleating louder than the lad in there was.

I could strip. I didn't mind baring it all. I'd convinced myself of that. And the Pride vids I'd watched had the boys doing just that. The naked lads holding each other. They didn't have sex. I'd even wank for the camera, but…?

My hands found the arms of the chair, my fingers curling around the metal tubes. I was going to push myself up and get to my feet. And I was going to walk smartly to the Underground station without looking back once. I was going to go back to Kings College and pretend this'd never happened. That I'd never been so stupid.

The outer door opened. I shuddered and released my grip on the chair arms. I didn't look up. I was too ashamed. "Are you waiting for an interview?" a man asked. It was a voice I was much too familiar with. Fearfully, I looked up. I was caught.

"Tim! What the bloody fuck?" Iain demanded as he had always done when he didn't approve of something I did.

"I could ask the same thing." I forced a smile to my face. "I think you misread the advert. They want versatile. Do you give more than one blowjob a year?"

"That hurt," he grumbled, blanching. "But then I deserve it. A lot more too, I suspect. How're you doing?"

"I'm—"

A squeal ran up the scale and was lost. I thought it was a different voice this time.

"My God! What the bloody hell are they doing in there?"

"I think they're planning to have their actors do more than the ones in Pride Videos do."

"How many lads are in there?"

"Just two and the director."

Iain rolled his eyes. "Are you staying then?"

"I thought I might," I told him, making a decision I hadn't expected. "And you? Are you actually going to let a bloke between your legs? Braveheart with the ever-virgin bum and nearly virgin mouth?"

He colored slightly and shrugged. "If it's the right bloke. I've grown up some, Tim." He looked down at his hands clasping each other in his lap. "I hope that you'll let me show you how much."

I began to move in on him. His hands came up to my neck and he pulled me down to him. Our lips touched and mine were parting to let his tongue in. I reached between us and found his cock. I pulled his skin up and began to rub his bared knob-end against my belly. He swelled in my hand.

The loneliness of the past year melted from me. The hurt was being buried deeper and deeper beneath the avalanche of pent-up pleasure cascading over and through me.

The lads exited the office rubbing their bums through their jeans. The bulges they sported suggested that the complaints we'd heard might have been a bit of bad acting. They colored crimson when they saw us and shuffled shamefacedly to the door. One held back a moment and turned to us. "We softened him up for you blokes," he told us cheekily. "It won't be a bad interview now." His mate grabbed his arm and pulled him through the door.

The big man named Max looked out the door and was quite obviously adjusting himself inside his trousers. "Ah," he said, "there's two of you now. And you seem to know each other as well. Come in then; let's chat."

He held out his hand and introduced himself again. "We're doing a film for America, lads," he said as he started towards his desk. "They like the complete thing over there, which means that you'll need to have sex in front of the camera. Do you think you can do that?"

I was suddenly undecided again. My resolve to be as daring as Iain was gone. I still wanted to leave, but I wanted to have Iain again too, even if it was only before a camera. "We can," Iain told him, cutting short my thoughts.

"Good. Well, let's cut to the chase. Let me see both of you naked. Then you can do the nasty for me, okay?"

After we stood naked in front of Max and after he'd felt both sides of both of us up, he nodded. "Yes, you will do very nicely indeed. Just the one thing more—I want to see you shag. I want to see that you want each other. Pass that test and you're signed on. Who's the top?"

Iain glanced over at me, an impish smile playing across his lips. "He is," he told Max and me.

"You two are perfect!" Max gushed from beside us. "I knew you were lovers when I saw you together. I'm going to rewrite the script so that it'll concentrate on you. You're going to be bloody stars!" Out of the corner of my eye, I could see him on his knees watching me wank Iain's fully erect prick while I fucked him.

"Bugger off!" Iain growled, breaking away from our kiss. "Can't you bloody well see that he's fucking me and I'm loving it?"

After we were in our clothes and on our way to the Underground with contracts in hand, I looked at Iain as we walked. "Want to come over to the flat for a pint?"

He chuckled. "Only if it's for the night, Tim. And only if we're shagging the whole time."

"One dose and you're addicted?"

"I think so. But we can be versatile, if you'd like."

Screen Test

Ruthless

"AM I REALLY A MOVIE PRODUCER, BABY?" I PURRED AT THE BIG handsome kid who had followed me as far as the studio door. "You bet your life I am. C'mon in here, kid, and I'll show you my casting couch."

When I met him in a fast food joint on Sunset Strip he told me his name was Billy Ray Hollister. I didn't think he would have given me the time of day if I hadn't told him that I was a Hollywood movie producer. He was about twenty-two years old, he was every inch of six feet and he had hair the color of straw and pale blue eyes the color of cornflowers. He had a husky voice that would have given me a hard-on, even if he hadn't had a build to die for. I was pretty sure he had a sock stuffed into the crotch of his tight, faded jeans—because, if he didn't, I was in love.

"Your castin' couch, sir?" he asked politely.

"Call me Sam, Billy Ray," I said. I took a key out of my pocket and unlocked the door that was labeled A & C Productions. Billy Ray had wide eyes. He hadn't been in California for very long yet. So what if the door was in a so-so neighborhood and led into a run-down building that had once been a paint warehouse? The sign on the door told him that movies were made here and he was thrilled to be given a guided tour.

We moved into the big, shadowed room. In one corner there was furniture set up to look like a living room. It might have been nothing more than a reception area set up for visitors to sit and wait, if it weren't for the tape marks on the floor. Billy Ray approached the furnished corner slowly.

Ordinarily at this time of day we would have been shooting. This was supposed to be the third day of production for *Ebony and Ivory* but Hans Memberg, the ivory, German half of our feature had snorted one too many lines of coke. When the crew was all assembled two hours earlier, Hans had just sat there smirking blearily at his chocolate-skinned co-star, his dick dangling. His eight-and-a-half-incher was hanging limply between his legs like laundry left out in the rain. All the Viagra in the world couldn't have given him a hard-on again. So, the day's work and probably the rest of the production had been canceled and I had gone off morosely in search of tacos.

"This here is the set for our latest production," I told him. "What do you think?"

His big blue serious eyes looked at the furniture thoughtfully. "It's a good set," he said. "It's supposed to be in some ordinary person's house, right? The furniture looks used and it's not very expensive."

He turned his head and flashed a smile down on me. "I think your set designers are pretty good! I watch sitcoms all the time about people who are supposed to be struggling to make ends meet. They all have huge houses with expensive furniture and it just doesn't look like they're ordinary folks at all."

Poor Billy Ray. He might be just in from the country but he wasn't dumb. He could see our set didn't look like a high-budget, low-reality sitcom. He thought our cheapskate set was a masterpiece because it looked like the real world. The truth is A & C productions buys its set furnishings from the Salvation Army. Tinsel on a shoestring budget. Not that A & C Productions doesn't rake the money in. Porn's a thriving industry. But God forbid we should spend more money to produce a film than we had to.

"That's right Billy Ray," I said. "Not all movies are glamorous, you know. Our latest production is kinda—" I paused. "Kinda a working man's movie. It's a realistic production."

His smile was almost blinding. "Can I sit down on the set?" I nodded and he put his square, handsome butt down carefully on one end of the couch. I sat beside him as close as I dared.

"It takes a lot of work and dedication to get into the movies," I warned him. "You got the looks, kid. No one can deny you that. But do you have the acting ability?"

"I think I do, Mr. Sam," Billy Ray told me earnestly. "I've had my heart set on acting a long time. I can really get into a role and be that character. I live that character when I'm acting."

"I sure would like to help you, Billy Ray." And I did want to help him. It's as real as can be, all the stories about good looking kids who come to Hollywood to act in the movies and just end up as hookers, working the strip. Good looks fade fast.

"I won't lie to you," I said. "I can't just make a phone call and get you a part. I wish I could. If I could, I would in a minute." I shook my head.

A big blond god like Billy Ray with his wide shy grin could have made every female heart in the country throb to see his smile on a screen. Just like he was making the forty-six-year-old heart of a short balding D-movie cameraman throb. And my groin too. I was starting to sweat.

His husky voice was wistful. "Even if you can't find me even a bit part, do you think you could at least give me a screen test, Mr. Sam?"

Damn! I wanted him so bad. Do you know what it's like to be short and hairy? I never get the hunky guys like Billy Ray. All the sit-ups in the world—I do a hundred and fifty sit-ups every morning, rain, shine or hangover, I don't even cheat on one—but I still have a potbelly. Nothing in the world is going to turn me into a good-looking stud at my age. If I go into a bar cruising, I might as well have a sign tacked on my forehead announcing "Troll." Yes, and another one on my back saying "Desperate." The good-looking guys, the broad-shouldered boys with the gleaming grins and the big baskets, they never look at me.

Billy Ray was different though. All it took was a lie, one word that I'd never labeled myself with before, and all the brilliance of a wheat field in the sun, concentrated in his smile, had been turned on me.

I'm not a producer you see. I'm a cameraman. Number one cameraman at A & C productions, what the hell is that worth? Once upon a time I dreamed about making the definitive documentary about the Civil War. I was going to have a name, I thought. Twenty years working and what did I have to show for it? A decent paycheck, that was all. I didn't have the connections to get this kid a part in a genuine movie. I didn't have the pull. I had nothing but desperation. They laughed at me in the bars downtown. "Shrimp." "Toad." That's what they called me.

That was why the lie had suddenly shot out of me, when Billy Ray turned his twenty-two-year-old golden gaze on me at the Taco-Whopper. "I'm a producer," I had said, somebody else in my body doing the talking. Suddenly his story had all come tumbling out in an unstoppable flood. He was new in town and he didn't have a place to stay, he was looking for a roommate. He had no idea that it would be so expensive to live here, it wasn't like Calgary. He thought he could be an actor, a really good actor, he was desperate to get into the movies, someway, somehow. "I'd do anything to get into the movies," Billy Ray had vowed to me. "Anything."

Lord, let me land this kid. Don't let this one get away, let me run my hands down his smooth skin, over those rock-solid muscles, bury my lips in the country-boy hair of his curly pubes. I'll do anything, I swore. I'll find him a place to crash. My apartment is big enough for a roommate, easy. I'll let him stay in my apartment, even if he loathes the very sight of me and it means I have to sleep in the car. I'll call everybody. I'll grovel on his behalf. I'll pay his way through acting school, but please let me land Billy Ray Big Cock just once and I'll never pray to get laid on a Saturday night again.

"I think you'd wow anybody with a screen test for sure, Billy Ray," I said.

He leaned toward me eagerly. "Can't you give me one now, Mr. Sam, right here? I'll show you how hard I'd work for you! I'll take any kind of a part at all! Anything!"

Anything, Billy Ray? He had said it again. A lump stuck in my throat. He'd do anything to get a part. And I would do anything to get his cock into my hands and mouth and butt, even lie my tongue off like the worst kind of a fucker in the world, the kind of fucker who would prey on the dreams of a kid from the provinces who's never been in the big city before.

I guess I stuttered a bit. "You won't necessarily get the kind of a part you'd like, Billy Ray. You might have to play some kind of a role that isn't the kind of character you've been hoping for."

"Sure, I understand that!" He nodded knowingly and hitched himself closer. "I expect to start small. I expect to play supporting roles."

"Or—" Lord, my throat was scratchy. "You might have to play a part or a character you didn't like, a character that wasn't really you. Say, maybe a gay guy or something."

He paused then, just for a moment. "Play the role of a gay guy? Like, try to act the part as if I was gay? I could even do that, Mr. Sam. Is that the screen test you want to give me?"

I moaned. He stood up, grabbed me by the shoulders and got me on my feet. "You just watch, Mr. Sam. I'm going to convince you that I'm gay! You're going to believe this!"

He stood back a pace and drew a breath. Suddenly a look came into his eyes. I don't know how to describe it. They became so intense that they blazed achingly bright blue like a prairie sky full of summer sun. His lips parted. He looked at me hungrily. "I want to fuck you," Billy Ray breathed in his husky voice. He gazed right at me, down at five-and-a-half-foot tall me and just for a moment his greedy, needy gaze made me feel like he really did want me.

"I'm gonna show you how much I want you, Mr. Sam," he said. "See this?" His thumb slid down in a slow stroke over that fat bulge in his jeans. It was just the thumb outside of the denim, but the lump in the cloth was so big it made his large thumb look small and that stroking motion was more erotic than when any other guy flashed everything he had. "Moment I laid eyes on you—" His voice was quiet. "I thought, here's a guy I'd like to wake up and find between my sheets, a guy I'd like to wake up in the morning by taking his cock in my mouth."

He opened the snap. "Do I give you a hard on, Mr. Sam?" The faint sound of his zip was like a roaring in my ears. I had words frozen in my mouth. I knew I had to stop him right here, right quick, because I didn't have a part I could offer him, and what would Billy Ray do when he found out he'd strutted his stuff for a nasty old con man who had strung him a line? He'd probably take those big square fists of his and pound the stuffing out of the nasty old con man in question—but, more than that, he'd feel like a dumb shit. My lips opened on the unsaid words.

He put two fingers to my lips and poked between them, rocking them slow like a cock going into a virgin's mouth. "Stop me if you don't want to hear it, Mr. Producer, because if you don't stop me, you're going to have one hell of a big horny man humping your ass in a moment—"

His jeans came down. There were no shorts, just a cock that my eye judged to be close to nine inches. Maybe a shade more. It must have been half crushed in those jeans. It pointed straight up at me, because Billy Ray was standing close and plucking at my shirt by now.

Oh, my poor, love-stricken heart! I'd seen a lot of cock in my profession. I'd seen them but I didn't get to touch them. I'd be lying if I said I'd ever seen one that looked finer. It was capped with a perfectly shaped head and as straight as an arrow—Cupid's arrow. Carry me away in your arms, Billy Ray, and fuck me with that awesome love tool forever! I really was in love.

He didn't act just with his voice. He acted with his hands. They moved on me with swift, barely controlled impatience. He looked and moved like he was itching to get the clothes off of me. He pulled my shirt down from my shoulders and when he saw the mat of dark and curly hair that covers my chest, his lips dove into it with a hungry gasp. His perfect white teeth nipped and tugged on my tits. The sensation was so distracting that, just for a moment, I didn't feel his hands on my zip.

Cold air on my hot cock warned me that he had found my hard-on. "Baby!" he breathed hoarsely. "Oh God, you are! You're just as fuzzy as I hoped you'd be." Evidently he was getting into the part enough not to be shocked to see that I was getting into the part too. In another moment he was on his knees at my feet. He grinned up at me now. He started lapping and slurping on my balls, taking them into his hand. "Mmmm, Sam. Your sweaty groin tastes delicious!"

Without taking his lips away or stopping the nibbling and licking that he was doing, Billy Ray began to tear his shirt down his shoulders. They were great, round shoulders, as wide as a prairie barn.

My hands came down and I filled my palms with his muscle. I had to try to pretend to be a producer. Try, I ordered myself. I struggled to find a voice. "Do you work out by lifting weights, Billy Ray?" I asked conversationally.

"No Sir, Mr. Sam. Not unless you count hay bales." He grinned. "I come by this muscle honestly." Then he demonstrated just how strong his muscle was. He picked me up and dumped me on my back on the couch. He gave a couple of quick tugs and my pants were clean gone. I was mother-naked. Billy Ray's gorgeous mouth was seeking and sucking between my legs.

He started to eat out my asshole. He pulled my cheeks wide to send his tongue hungrily poking. He lapped and slurped up and down. And all the while his blue eyes were gleaming at me over my crotch. "Does this prove to you how bad I want the part, Mr. Sam?"

"Guh," I admitted. I'd lost the ability to talk. I didn't have to. While he rimmed my asshole, he wrapped his hard, strong hands about my prick and worked it up and down. He took my groan for encouragement to go on. His tongue burrowed deep into my crack.

Just when I thought he'd bring me over the edge he took his hand away from my prick and he rose up over me again. He loomed over me, his fair hair falling over his forehead. "I think it's time I got this fat cock of yours up my butt," he told me. My eyes rolled up like I'd been sandbagged.

There was just one moment in his role playing when he hesitated. He pulled away from me just after he said he wanted my cock in his ass. This was it. Mute despair. For a moment my stomach plunged sickeningly with disappointment. He'd taken it as far as he could stomach it, I thought. But then he was fumbling in his shirt pocket and I saw that his hesitation was only because he was pausing to get a rubber out.

He squatted over me. His face was intent as he rolled the condom down my cock. And then he sank down sitting on my lap, easing his butt open, sinking down on me and letting my prick grind up into the depths of his ass.

I didn't have to do anything. He rocked up and down letting my cock ride like a piston into his tight, clamping hole. Up and down. Up and down. I cupped his dick with my hands whimpering with the sheer pleasure of it.

There was a noise, just to one side of us—the squeak of dolly wheels. I saw Billy Ray's head snap sideways at the faint sound. It was Freddie Kaiser, our grip, trundling one of the big spotlights into place at the edge of the set. I hadn't even noticed that he had come into the big room, and Freddie wasn't paying any attention to us either. Two guys fucking were just scenery to him.

Billy Ray looked down at me. His voice was even as he made ready to pull off of my prick. "You want an audience?" he asked. He jerked his head meaningfully at Freddie. He was telling me that if I wanted him to, he would make Freddie go away. And I didn't doubt he could and would do it. There was such force and confidence in his strong, young body.

"He works here," I mumbled.

I tried to think how I could explain to Freddie if a big, naked, golden Canadian boy suddenly rushed him off the set. But Billy Ray was willing to let it go if I was. He nodded. A faint smile curved his mouth as he resumed his ride on my groin. "If you get turned on by an audience, you can have one," said Billy Ray

Only by now, Freddie had picked up on the fact that Billy Ray was the only guy on the couch with the hard-muscled, smooth body of a screen god—that and that there were two of us. He had noticed me. "Hey!" he blurted, "Sam! What're you doing?"

"He's giving me a screen test," Billy Ray answered, perfectly self-assured as he got back to riding me. He never saw the stupefied expression come over Freddie's face. Billy Ray turned his eyes back down on me as easily as that and he paid no more attention again to anything that went on behind him.

He rode me. Into the sunset like an old western. His cock jerked and bounced as I slid in and out of him. My balls tightened. I was getting closer.

Dollies soon squeaked. For a moment. A light dazzled, then muted. "Screen test for the blond?" I heard the distant baffled murmur of Paulie Harris's voice as my balls churned. Paulie was a producer while I was not. It was Paulie who produced and directed one half of A & C; he had sole control of the Ass & Cock division which puts out the gay porn.

Paulie Harris was going to think I was trying to pass myself off as him. This could mean my job. I blew the biggest load of my life up Billy Ray's butt. My heart palpitated. I gasped. And I shot more jizz. I was definitely in love—if I lived long enough to express it.

But Billy Ray was leaning over me, pulling off me, and his wide, bright grin filled up my sight while his big hand went around my prick and pulled off the rubber. I forgot about Paulie Harris. This was my only moment. As long as Billy Ray was still suckered in by my lie I could feel the way it felt to have a man fierce with horniness for me. I filled my senses with him and ignored the rest.

He flung himself down on me and bit and nibbled at my throat and tits. He pushed my knees back so he leaned between them and his cock was pressed on mine. Its hot length throbbed. "You wanta be fucked, Sam?" he whispered. "You want my cock driving in your hairy ass?"

I nodded eagerly. He used his mouth while he got a rubber in place on his prick. Camera? Yeah, there was a camera somewhere. There was the quick click of a light meter and maybe a camera lens pushed up somewhere near my butt. No way was I going to be distracted by a camera, not while Billy Ray was placing the head of his prick to my hole, ready to impale me.

He teased me with it. He placed it against me and grinned, waiting for me to beg. I begged instantly. "Fuck me, Billy Ray! Fuck me now! Let me have it! Shove your cock up my ass!"

He rammed it home and all the pleasure-pain of his thick, thrusting fuck-tool was mine. He held my legs back and rammed his fat, hard cock in my ass. He was reared up tall. Sweat gleamed on his chest as his hard thrusts pounded home into me. He battered into me, the full length of his meat sliding in until I felt his heavy balls flattening against me at the deep end of every stroke. He was holding my legs up. He looked like he was on the edge of cumming himself, but for long minutes, he kept it up until my prick was weeping pre-cum.

Billy Ray leaned down again. He still held my leg back so that my ass was turned up to meet his fierce, steady strokes. But he put his mouth on mine. His tongue slid between my lips. I strained up to meet the kiss. His hand tightened on my prick. It thrummed. It flew hard and fast. His cock kept working, plowing me rhythmically.

When I started groaning, he groaned back. We were gasping right into each other's lips. I felt the sweet, hot surge of cum burst up and out of me, spurting through his finger and thumb. At the same moment he timed it so he came himself. I felt his cock pulsing like an earthquake inside me as he came deep in my ass.

His chest was heaving as he pulled slowly back. He didn't pull out of me, but gave me more room to breathe. Those two young eyes looked down in hopeful expectancy. He was waiting for me to say something, but I was too spent to do anything but lie there, flat out on my back.

"Cut!" The clatter of the crew around us brought me from my daze. Billy Ray raised his head again and looked at the ring of guys who surrounded us.

"What's your name, Fella?" Paulie Harris roared. "You got the job!"

"You mean this was a real screen test? For real?" Billy Ray's blue eyes went wide again. He pulled back out of me and sprang to his feet off the couch. "Oh Lord, I am sorry! I'm not looking for an acting job. I don't need a job. I'm a law student at UCLA."

He looked around at the crew, then down at me with consternation on his face. "I just wanted the chance to have a fuck with you, Mr. Sam. I thought you were leading me on about helping me find a part. I didn't mean to lead you on."

I couldn't have said a word to save my life. I was struck as dumb as a billboard, but Paulie Harris wasn't operating under my handicap. He exploded.

"What? Nine-and-two-thirds fucking cut inches, you make the goddamn camera sizzle for fuckssake, you'll even pork a troll like Sammy without bitchin' that his balls need a hair cut and you're not interested in taking the part? I do not fuckin' believe it! I know it ain't the crowd on the set! What is it? Why don't you want the job!?"

"I told you. I'm not looking for work." Billy Ray still had a startled expression on his face.

"Kid, take the job! There's a bonus in it for you. A big bonus. We need a blond boy like you to play the opposite in our latest feature.

Five days' work, that's all. You can finish me off this production on your Thanksgiving break, another one at Christmas. Don't break my fucking heart, I gotta have you."

I drew my legs down at this point. Nobody paid attention to me. We spend a lot of time not noticing naked guys on the sets at A & C Productions. Nobody spared me an eyeball. As I pulled my clothes on Billy Ray was still shaking his head at Paulie Harris: "Well, yes, it is pretty decent money and it would pay for next semester, but I had no idea—"

Paulie went right on arguing: "Kid, if I have to beg, I'll beg! Jock Jamal is a ton more good looking that Sam the Shrimp. You can have the pick of your co-stars."

I would have left, but Freddie pulled me aside and asked me what agency had sent this blond superstud over to us. He was looking as gloomy as a basset hound. "Paulie never asked me to give an audition to any of the actors," he complained. I didn't see how the conversation between Billy Ray and Paulie Harris ended. I knew I wouldn't be doing any camera work today, so as soon as I could pry myself lose from Freddie's questions, I headed for the door.

I was on the sidewalk already and starting on the long walk home when I heard him shout. "Wait!" Billy Ray came running up behind me with his shirt untucked. He was still putting his clothes together as he ran. I stopped.

"I'm real sorry for lying to you that I was looking for an acting job like that, Sam," he told me. "But when you told me that you were in the movie business, it sounded to me like something from a b-movie, I just got carried away. I didn't mean to do it."

"That's okay, Billy Ray," I told him, my voice expressionless. I was back to being Sammy the cameraman. Sammy the Troll.

He dropped into step beside me, while he tucked in his shirt tails. "There's one thing I did tell the truth about, if you're not too mad at me." He grinned hopefully and shamefacedly at once. "Thing is, I really am still looking for a roommate and a place to stay—"

I stopped and stared at him. My heart started to beat again. With happiness. With hope.

Crashers

Alex Corey

JASON AND I WORRY THAT WE'LL NEVER BE DISCOVERED WITH THIS fluorescent lighting, but that's all there is at the Bingo Kwik-Print. It adds a sickly bluish-green tint to Jason's black hair and makes every freckle on my face look as though I'm painted up for a circus act.

Jason and I run the graveyard shift, so by the time we're ready to go home, we're both usually too worn-down to look screen-worthy. Jason tries to compensate by wearing white T-shirts so tight that I can tell which nipple rings he's wearing. I've got a ridiculous cast on my arm and the whole thing is in a sling from a recent biking accident.

Right now, Jason is helping Patsy Simmons print out her latest mystery novel so she can send it out to every publisher in America while I stand like an idiot behind the register. I watch two men step out of a building across the street and look my way.

The taller one holds a sheaf of papers while the other one, older and somewhat stocky, gestures wildly, pointing at me a lot. The stocky man turns back inside the building; the taller man looks up and down the street, then dashes across and into the store. He checks out Jason and Patsy, then approaches me at the counter.

The man is much younger than he appeared outside, probably twenty-five tops, and cute to boot. If I could scratch behind his ears, I'd bet I'd find baby fuzz.

"You do rush jobs here?" he asks.

It's a line Jason could work to full advantage, but I just get tongue-tied and mutter: "Uh, sure—"

"Good." He sets the papers down on the countertop and spreads them out. Most are photos of naked men; a few of the faces I recognize from Jason's magazines and videos, along with a few of the cocks. "You do this kind of work here?" he asks. "You're okay with this?" His accent is some smooth European hybrid, Italian and Scandinavian at the same time.

"Sure. I'll do them."

He looks at me with serious brown eyes. "It's for an invitation. A party. We need to put these—" he points to the photographs— "on these." He points to the sheets of paper he brought with him. "Then we shrink them down to postal card size and print them on colors so they can't be copied. You can do this?"

I scan the photos, hoping that the man himself might be featured among them. I've already undressed him in my mind, but I'd still like to see proof of my assumptions: the hairless chest, the flat, light pink nipples, the screw-head belly button, the trail of dark brown hair leading from it to his uncut cock. Jason says I'm a sexual psychic that way; I always know whether a man is cut or uncut, smooth or hairy, an innie or an outie.

"I can definitely do this," I tell him.

"Good. Here is my number. I am right across the street. You call me when you're ready." He pushes his business card across the counter like it's the missing card in a magic trick. "How long do you think?"

I'd guess six or seven inches, but I fight back the urge to say it. "An hour. Tops."

"Tops," he says. He smiles at me. "Tops. I like you. You're a good boy, very funny. Tops."

Jason finally helps Patsy get her copies to her car and rushes over. "Who was that hunk in here a few minutes ago?" He doesn't even wait for an answer; he just snatches up a sheet of the invitations as they spit out of the copier.

"Jesus Christ," he says in amazement, looking at the picture.

"No, I think that's Paul Morgan. I can't remember. Does Paul Morgan bend to the left or the right when he's hard?"

"What the hell are these?" Jason asks.

"Invitations. Some party for the company across the street. I guess they're movie producers. Porno movies." I hold up another invitation that shows Brent Woodin taking it up the ass. His famously thick lips form a perfect circle of ecstasy while Giorgio Priccotti arches underneath him and thrusts upward, a trademark position that makes his spectacular abs look like venetian blinds.

Jason takes the invitation from me and reads it out loud. "Get Balled at the Ball... Masquerade... All the top actors... All the top producers..." He looks up at me. "This is amazing. How many of these are you making?"

"A hundred. For all the top actors—and maybe a few of the bottoms, too."

Jason smiles, though I can't be sure if it's because he likes the idea of bottoms at a party or if there's something else on his mind. He points to his head and says: "Brilliant idea."

"Warning alarm," I say and point to his crotch.

"Print up some extras," Jason says. "We're going."

"What do you mean we're going? We can't crash a porno party!"

"Oh yes we can." He takes a sheet of invitations over to the paper cutter. "The address is right here on the card."

"I can't believe you're serious."

"Believe. Believe."

Across the room, Jason turns back and forth in front of a mirror and makes final adjustments to his pirate outfit. He wears a black bandanna on his head, tight black leather pants, and a billowing white sleeveless shirt open all the way down the front. Tiny daggers dangle from his ear, and when he turns a certain way, I can see the small sword replica piercing his left nipple. He has shoved another sword, plastic but life-size, into his pants and admires the illusion of some serious meat down there.

I'm standing in my briefs, trying to figure out a way to put my own costume on with only one functional arm. After several botched attempts, I look over at Jason with my best puppy-dog frown. "Ask a favor?"

Jason stops modeling in front of the mirror and comes over. I hand him the roll of gauze I've been fumbling with. "You're absolutely positive this guy will recognize you?" he asks me. "I mean, this seems a bit extreme."

I lift up my arm in its cast. "Jason, I think even you'd agree that this qualifies as a distinguishing feature by now."

"Okay. You're the boss." He bends down and wraps the end of the gauze around my ankle and ties it off, then begins to unroll the rest up and around my calves, being careful when he gets to the knees to give me some degree of flexibility. From there he moves up around the thighs. "I'm just going to keep on going and not tell you how horny this is making me," he says as he brings the roll around my butt and then in front to cover my crotch.

"Oh, please," I say with teasing sarcasm. Even so, with Jason squatting in front of me and his hands hovering around my crotch, my cock stiffens a bit and I can feel my balls shift around in the pouch of my briefs.

"You just hold on down here," Jason says, "or I'm gonna have to go out and get more gauze."

"Sorry," I say. Jason stands up and backs away slightly, still staring at my briefs as my cock presses even harder against the fabric and pushes apart several layers of gauze.

"All hands to the mizzenmast," he says. He drops the roll of gauze and reaches down to wrap his fingers around my cock and balls, then gives a squeeze. I wince, surprised by both the speed and force of his gesture. With my uninjured arm, I push his hand away.

In our five years of living together in three different apartments, Jason has never touched me like that. He has tickled me when I was topless, pulled a towel away after a shower, and given me some deeply satisfying bare-back massages, but neither he nor I have ever touched one another in the "forbidden zone." That doesn't mean I didn't look at him when he came into the bathroom and peed while I brushed my teeth, or didn't have mild fantasies whenever I caught him napping naked on the couch. Once I even tiptoed across the floor to study his body as he lay there: the bird-like pattern his chest hair made as it spread across both nipples, the adorable way his penis lay flat back against his belly and nestled like a pet in his thatch of black pubic hair.

"If you don't learn to control yourself, sailor, I may have to deny your request for shore leave," Jason says. He pulls the sword out of his pants and pokes the tip in my navel for emphasis. It's somewhat sharp despite being plastic, and I twist around from the mixed jolts of pleasure and pain. He then lets the point drop down, bisecting the diamond-shaped patch of hair above my crotch. When the tip reaches the waistband of my briefs, he lifts his arm high and angles the sword downward, pushing the shaft slowly inside so that I can feel the blade against my prick. He jiggles the sword around a bit, then withdraws it. "Arrr, that's a serious saber you've got down there, matey. Would ye mind if I borrowed it for the night?"

With his sword he skewers the roll of gauze and lifts it up off the floor so that I can grab it. "You'd better cover that spot up," he says, and taps the edge of the blade against the front of my underwear. I look down to see that a small drop of precum has seeped through the pouch. When I look back, Jason is licking the blade where it touched me. He smacks his lips and winks. "You're a tasty morsel," he says, "salty as the sea. If I weren't setting sail for a wild party, I'd drop me anchor right here."

For a moment I can't tell if Jason is being serious or just playing the part of lusty pirate again. I can, however, tell that the bulge in his leather pants is real this time, and it's all I can do to keep from suggesting that he use my ass as a sheath.

The party takes place in a sprawling villa overlooking the ocean; shirtless studs at the gate take our invitations and tell us where to park. We arrive around midnight, when we're certain that most of the guests will already be there. We can tell we're making some kind of impression with our late entrance; heads turn as we drive past the main entrance to the parking area. The black feathers in Jason's pirate hat whip around above his head, while my mummy costume glows conspicuously in the moonlight.

When we get inside, I'm amazed by the huge platters of food that fill several banquet tables. More shirtless staff members stand at the ready behind rows of overturned champagne glasses. Most of the guests are gathered around the tables nibbling on the peeled baby carrots. I notice that the broccoli has gone untouched on virtually every platter; one can never be too careful about a stray floret between the teeth when trying to make an impression.

Jason comes up beside me after a few minutes and nudges my good arm. He wants me to compliment him on the amount of food he has assembled on one plate.

From the moment we arrived at the party, I've realized that my costume was a huge mistake. Jason had wrapped me up tightly, almost vengefully, with both arms against my chest for what he called "authenticity." Now I'm entirely reliant on him to lift both food and drink to my lips, and will no doubt have to ask for his assistance whenever I have to take a leak, which, given my rather nervous state, will be soon.

"Those guys at the salad bar asked me who you were," Jason says. He points at them with a sliver of green pepper, then lifts the crisp piece to my mouth. White ranch dressing smears across my lower lip, but Jason goes on talking without noticing. "I told them it was a secret. Told them if anyone knew who you were, there'd be no keeping the boys off you."

"Thanks," I say, still chewing on the pepper. "A little help here—"

Jason looks up to see the dribble. "Sexy," he says. He dabs his index finger against my lip and wipes the dressing away, then inserts the finger into my mouth so that I can lick it clean. "Just a taste of things to come," he says with a wink.

Across the room, the group of men watches us intently. Like most of the models and actors assembled, they're clad in scanty costumes—jungle boys and Indian braves, Greek slaves and Olympians, anything to show off their well-oiled pecs and crunch-hardened abs. What clothing they do wear is generally mesh or gauze and leaves little to the imagination as they pose themselves. When the track lighting hits him just right, I can tell that Tarzan sports a silver cock ring behind his loin cloth; a black Spartacus has opted for leather with what appear to be brass studs glinting beneath the see-through tunic.

By contrast, the industry execs in the room are all gussied-up in lavish outfits. Gold-lined capes and shimmering hoop skirts abound, along with corsets and epaulets meant to enhance the aging features of former-stars-turned-directors. I realize that, like the bigwigs and insiders in the room, I've chosen concealment over exposure with my costume, and have been gawking at all the half-naked bodies more like a buyer than someone with something to sell.

"I vant to suck your cum," says a vampire who has come up beside me. He raises the sides of his cape in a swoosh and tries to envelop the two of us in its black satin realm, but only succeeds in knocking a tray of salmon puffs out of the hands of a passing waiter. The pleasant shock of seeing Dracula's powdered torso and abs is lost as both he and Jason stoop to help the waiter pick up the pastries. I stand stock-still, suddenly thankful for the way the gauze around my head masks my embarrassment.

As he bends over, Jason's sword reaches back and knocks against my ankles. I notice the way the black leather stretches across the two lobes of his ass, a beautifully wrapped package, and how a thin, barely visible patch of hair floats like a puff of smoke at the base of his spine.

Dracula stands up and tosses the sides of his cape back over his shoulders. "Sorry, mate," he says in an English accent. I look down at his chest, smooth and pale, with two of the plumpest, reddest nipples I've ever seen. "I'm afraid I'm no bloody good in a crowd," the Count continues. "But if you'd like, I can show you a trick or two in private." He leans in close and nibbles at my ear, or at least where he thinks my ear might be. "I know a thing or two about res-erection," he whispers.

"Maybe later," Jason says, suddenly coming between Dracula and me. "Right now I think Mr. Z. would like to get a drink. If you'll excuse us—?" He puts his hand on my ass and guides me away from Dracula's bared fangs and stake-like nipples.

"Well, wasn't that original," Jason says once we're out of earshot. He sounds rather annoyed, almost hurt or offended.

"Were you jealous?" I ask.

"Of that vamping queen? Please."

"I mean that he came on to me instead of to you," I explain.

Jason stops to look at me with a slightly puzzled expression, then turns away. I can feel his hand on my ass, even after he takes it away to guide me by the shoulder. "We need champagne," he says as he scans the room. "You stay here. And don't talk to any more strangers."

He heads over to a makeshift bar where three other men wait for drinks. A mirror behind the bar lets me watch his expression, now somewhat nervous despite his earlier bravado. I can also catch a reflection of myself, and realize for the first time how the tight-fitting gauze flatters my shoulders and ass and emphasizes the forward thrust of my cock and balls. Thin lines of skin are exposed where the strips have shifted, particularly around my mid-section.

This fact is not lost on Tarzan, who has been staring at my ass as he followed me across the room. His long blond hair sways as he walks toward me; his bare torso is lean and incredibly long, his stomach well-tuned and platter-shaped. I turn away from the mirror to face him.

"Looking for something to swing on?" I ask him, a bit shocked by my own boldness.

"You're coming undone," he says.

He reaches a finger down to my belly and lightly touches the skin that's exposed there. As he rubs his knuckle back and forth, he pushes down on the next strip to reveal my navel.

"You're an outie," he says.

He twirls his finger and pokes at the crescent-shaped nub with the tip.

My navel has always been my most sensitive "on" button, and often functions like a catch-release for my penis, which now strains against my briefs and the gauze Jason had wrapped tightly around it. Tarzan's other hand reaches down to press against the tension, and before I can say a thing he has pressed his mouth against mine and pushed past my lips with his tongue. I can taste the champagne he has been drinking, along with the faint, smoky flavor of the salmon puffs.

"Excuse me," someone says, and I feel a hand reaching between Tarzan and me, then a spill of cool liquid down my front. When Tarzan steps away, Jason is standing there, a glass held out in his hand. A thin film of champagne has spilled along Tarzan's front, glistening across the ridges of his abdomen and soaking his loin cloth so that it now clings quite revealingly to the curve of his hardened cock.

"Sorry," Jason says.

He sets the half-emptied glass on a nearby table and picks up some napkins, then wipes at Tarzan's stomach and loincloth, nearly shredding the napkins as well as the loincloth in the process. When it appears that the ape-man's full glory is about to be let loose in the room, Tarzan reaches down to cover himself and dash away.

"Real smooth," I say.

"Who, him?" Jason asks.

"No, you. That was Tony Manolo, you idiot."

"The one with the pinwheel stuck up his butt in *Studs and Stripes*?'" Jason asks.

"Yeah. The only guy who ever took every inch of Derek Jacobus, first down the throat, and then up the ass."

"I guess I haven't studied my pornstar trading cards as much as you." Jason wipes at my front, where wet strips of gauze have begun to sag and peel away from my skin, wrecking my costume.

"Let's see if we can find a place to get you all tidied up." Once more his hand grabs my ass, and he guides me through the crowd.

We pass down a hallway with a number of locked doors, then turn down another hallway, heading toward a separate wing of the house. We find a door that's been left open and duck inside, closing it behind us.

Jason feels around for a light switch but can't find one. That doesn't matter much; moonlight pouring in through a large skylight sets me aglow in the middle of the room. The light spreads like quicksilver over a massive, king-size bed, and I wonder if we've stumbled into the owner's bedroom.

"Well, here we are."

"Here we are," Jason repeats. "How's your arm?"

I try to lift it up, but it hardly moves. Even so, the motion causes wet strips of gauze to slip further down across my belly. "I'm getting kind of cramped in here."

"It's kind of weird, how jealous I felt out there." Jason's voice is serious in a tender, touching way. "How much I wanted you. Want you."

I can barely see him through the thin eye holes of my costume, but I feel him hovering nearby like a tangible shadow. Suddenly his hands brush up against my stomach, and his fingers slip between the gauze and skin. He tugs at the strips, and though they stretch out and loosen, they don't break. He leans forward and pulls at a strip with his teeth, his hair brushing against my belly as the fabric tears.

Jason tilts his head upward, moving first his forehead and then his nose across the tiny bulge of my navel. He rips the strips from my mid-section as he licks at my belly button, then takes the fold of skin between his teeth and gently nibbles.

Layer by layer, my costume unravels, first from delicate gestures of undress, then from frantic clawing as Jason paws at my crotch and yanks the fabric from around my legs. When he reaches my knees, he presses his mouth against my lower stomach and covers me with little wet kisses.

Jason grabs hold of the waistband of my briefs and pulls down slowly, following with his lips. Finally, just as my cock springs free of my underwear, his mouth captures it. He moves his head back and forth as though he might shake me by my member, then slows and lets the head of my prick rest on his tongue. The walls of his mouth wrap around me as he sucks the precum from my shaft. I can almost taste it myself as the tip of his tongue licks at the slit on my dickhead.

While Jason works on my cock, I adjust my arms inside the costume so that my fingers can brush against my nipples. They're already hard and aroused and somewhat moist from sweat, so I flick at them with my nails before taking them between my fingertips and twisting. Jason's hands reach up across my folded forearms and for a moment we're both twisting at the fleshy tits, fighting one another for a good strong grip.

I let him take over so that I can work my good arm down out of its gauzy cocoon. Once freed, I push the strips around my chest up and over my shoulder, then do the same on the other side. Meanwhile, Jason pulls on my nipples. He lets my spit-covered cock slip out of his mouth and spatter against his chest, then lets it slide along the length of his breastbone and stomach as he stands up in front of me.

"I have been waiting so long for this," he tells me. He lets go of my nipples and reaches up to unwrap my head. He does this carefully, gently, like someone unveiling a painting or statue. I feel both flattered and amazed by his tenderness.

Once my face is exposed, he presses his lips against mine. I'm overcome by how soft and warm they feel, like slept-on pillows.

"Jason puffs," I say, tasting once again the smoky seafood-flavor of the hors d'oeuvres. I pretend to bite into his lip and feel him smile before he steps away, back into shadow.

"What?" I ask after a moment.

"You look so beautiful in the moonlight," he says. "Almost translucent." He reaches out into the light and strokes my chest, then presses a fingertip against the left nipple. I realize that I am now naked except for my white sneakers, socks, and cast.

Jason reaches down and squeezes my cock. We both watch in wonder as a glimmering drop of precum forms on the tip and then swings slowly downward on a strand of web. Before it can touch the floor, Jason ducks under it and lets it slip into his mouth. He follows the strand back up to my prick and begins to suck hard.

I reach down to stroke his hair, shiny and black like fractured reflections of moonlight and night. I reach for the collar of his shirt and pull up; he raises his arms like wings behind him so that the sleeves can slide up along his arms and be lifted away.

"Keep them up," I whisper, and reach out to hold his wrists together once the shirt has been tossed aside. I let my hand slip down along his forearm, over the rough folds of his elbow, then around the smooth curve of his biceps, the padded muscles of his shoulder, and from there around front and under the arm, a shallow depression which deepens as I tickle the moist hairs tangled there. I carry the wetness on my fingertips as I rub against his nipple, rolling the skin back and forth across the tiny sword inserted there.

Jason continues to suck vigorously on my cock, his broad tongue wrapping itself around the head and savoring every pulled-out drop of precum. When I can feel myself tensing toward orgasm, I step back to the end of the bed—slowly, so that Jason can follow, my cock still held tight in his mouth. I lean back, tensing all the muscles in my body, reveling as he rubs his hands and forearms all up and down my chest and abs. Everything tingles at once: my tight nipples, my navel, my balls, my cock—even my asshole, which Jason has now found with his fingers. First one and then another squirms up inside me and starts me to quivering.

Jason's mouth tightens into a smile around my cock. He can probably tell by the way my ass clenches around his knuckles that I'm about to come, so he pulls my dick out of his mouth and with his free hand directs the shaft upward, jerking so hard that I swear he's trying to touch the tip to my chin.

When I come, I imagine hitting the moon in the window above me; I imagine the moon made liquid and spitting from my cock; I imagine myself as the moon and drenching Jason's body as he slides first his chest up and across my wet and throbbing cock, then his belly, pressing and pushing so that he can feel the hard pulse of my orgasm against his stomach. As the final shudders radiate through my body, Jason unclasps his buckle and shoves his tight leather pants down. Even in the silvery half-light, I can tell he's not wearing underwear, and watch in delight as his cock unfurls and slaps against his inner thigh.

"Can I?" he asks, already pulling at his stiffening shaft.

"Aye aye, captain," I say. "Come aboard."

Jason grabs his hat off the floor and pulls out a condom he has cleverly tucked in the band. I help him roll it down the shaft of his cock, anxious to feel his rod's thickness and length, grasping it in my hand to confirm what I thought all along: eight-and-a-half inches of what feels like five pounds. Jason reaches up and smears moonlit cum all over my front, then lubes his dick with it. He gently turns me around, careful not to knock against my bad arm, then waits for me to steady myself against the bed.

He starts in slow, just nudging the tip of his cock against the rim of my ass until he can feel the outer muscles loosen further. Next I can feel the head pushing in, pulling out, pushing in a bit deeper, pulling out, pushing in again, deeper still, then pushing deeper, and all the while I'm thinking it's my own glowing cum slicked around his sweet, pumped-up cock, and suddenly he's there and the moon is inside me, infusing my prostate with light.

Jason moves his hips in a circular motion so that his dickhead can massage the gland, then he slides in and out of me in a slow screw. I can feel his fingers tugging at his scrotum, moving forward to slap at my own whenever he thrusts deep. When he leans forward, I can tell where his nipples are against my back by the hard cool touch of the sword. I picture his own navel, small and star-shaped, brushing against the base of my spine.

Jason surrounds me with his arms, perhaps to pull me that much closer when he digs way down, perhaps to hold me together so I won't buckle from the force and heat of his thrusting cock. His hands caress me, first his palms across my pecs, then the backs of his hands across my underbelly. Just as I feel he is about to come, his thumb finds the knob of my navel and pushes up, pushes so that I am certain I can feel the head of his cock against the back of it, pushes so that he can work it around and massage his own dickhead deep inside of me. He times the thumb-prodding to match his final surges, huge spasms that leave us both crying out, our shrieks of delight as intermingled as our bodies.

The cries turn to laughter, then to sobs of joy as Jason slips his cock out of me. I can feel it dangling behind me, already softening against my buttcheeks. He holds me in a half-embrace as he pulls the condom off, then lets his cum-slick cock press against me once more.

Someone begins to clap in a corner of the room, slowly at first, then with greater speed and force. "Bravissimo," says a man. "This was beautiful, quite beautiful. I am very impressed." I recognize the accent; it is the man who came into the shop with the invitations. Jason and I stand up and face one another.

I hear a zipper being pulled up, then the creak of a chair as the man rises and steps toward the two of us. "I send you contracts tomorrow," the man says. "You'll be in my next film, the two of you. For now, though, I leave you to each other, as it should be."

Light spills into the room as he opens the door and leaves. I lie back on the bed, bathing in the moonlight as my semen dries on my skin. Jason reaches out to touch some of the still-wet spots reflecting the light. "Does that mean we get to do this again?" he asks.

"I'm holding out for a lifetime contract," I say.

"Where do I sign?"

"Right here." I point toward my chest.

"You want me to sign your cast?"

"We are the cast, sweetheart," I say.

Jason crawls up and over me on the bed. He takes his cock and squeezes out the last bit of jism, then grabs his dick by the head and begins to move it in graceful arcs across my stomach. As he signs his name on my skin, I can smell his semen mixing with my own.

"Consider it a done deal." Then, with one final flourish, Jason underlines his name with a wet and wonderful smear.

Special Talent

Dominic Santi

EVERYBODY WANTS MY DICK.

I'm the man with the connections: Jed Piper, of Backstage Casting. The company provides "special talent" to the star makers. I select the studs who make up that stable of talent. The young bucks know they have to make it past me to get to the goodies. Which means first they have to make it past my dick.

It's a beaut: 10 and 9/16 inches, trimmed, tapered, well-maintained by the hordes of wannabe pornstars who flock to my auditions. They hand me neat portfolios of their pictures and their vita sheets. I unzip and point them towards my meat. Not many have what it takes to be a Backstage man.

Most of them end up as fluffers. The big studios are always looking for hot new talent to keep their big name stars looking sharp. A good fluffer will always be in demand if he can keep a well-hung bottom-boy hard enough to fuck. If a punk gets me off during an audition, I try to turn him on to some sort of job in the industry.

Zack would have sucked dick just for the fun of it. He didn't care much about the pay, which was lousy to begin with. He just wanted a steady supply of hot, hard dicks to swallow. Getting paid to fall on his knees and worship his favorite screen stars was his dream come true.

He showed up in my office one hot August day—neat portfolio under his arm, shy, innocent smile. They get jaded early in this town. Zack was fresh meat, hot off the bus from Bakersfield. He'd shot most of his travel wad on his pictures. Good poses, I had to admit. They showed off his sparkling baby blues, well-sculpted pecs, and cute bubble butt to perfection. With his short, blond clone haircut, he could have been any face in the crowd. Except for his smile. It was so damned innocent. So naive. He was definitely somebody who needed my touch—someone I could mold into what I knew would be a damn fine pornstar.

"I've always dreamed of being an actor," he gushed the first time I met him. That certainly made me sit up and take notice. Most of these guys know when they walk through the door that acting is not required. "I'll do whatever it takes to work with the stars."

"I know you will," I smiled. My dick was already snaking down my leg. I didn't pretend to hide what I was doing as I rubbed myself through the pale linen of my Italian summer suit.

Zack licked his lips. "I'm v-very impressed with your credentials, sir," he stammered.

"Everyone is," I smiled condescendingly. "The question now is, what can you do for me? Why should Backstage Casting take a chance with a no-name like you?"

"Perhaps I could show you." He stopped and swallowed hard. His eyes were glued to the massive erection tenting the front of my trousers. "I'll do anything to be in movies, sir. Whatever it takes."

I shoved my chair back from my desk the rest of the way and patted my lap. "I know you will. Give me a quick sample of your talents, stud. Show me your stuff, and I'll see what positions I have on the books."

"Thank you, sir." He was on his knees, on the carpet, between my legs, so fast I barely saw him move. With one practiced movement, he slid my zipper down. He eased my throbbing cock out of my too-tight (by then) pants. I barely saw his hand move to his own pocket. The next thing I knew, I heard the quick sound of a wrapper tearing, and he was using his mouth to roll a condom down my tube.

I was surprised that he'd known to bring an extra-large, then glad he'd bothered to do his homework. The sheath was hot and tight as it slowly encased my massive tool. And that punk knew how to use his mouth. As soon as he had me dressed for company, he chowed down.

Fuck, he was good. He knew how to go slow. How to build up the tension, one slow lick at a time. He started at the base and worked his way up, touching, stroking, using his tongue and lips until I was breathing hard in spite of myself. Until I almost forgot I was a hard-ass casting professional doing an audition. This was one talented cock-sucker. Then he pulled out the pièce de résistance: he took my cock all the way down his throat. Just like some sword swallower from a fucking circus, he swivelled around, tipped his head back, opened his throat, and I felt his lips against my balls.

"Fuck!" I shot. I couldn't fucking help myself. He let himself gag just enough to make a quivering hot fuck tunnel in his throat. I yelled so hard they probably heard me in the cafeteria down the hall.

A moment later, he bobbed back up, pulling the rubber off me on his way past. As my cum dripped down onto the rug, Zack winked one of those sparkling baby blues at me. "Did I pass round one, sir?"

"Fuck, yes," I panted. My dick knew potential when I saw it. I was impressed.

I sent Zack out to the reception area to get me some coffee as I zipped back up. By the time he came back in, I'd had time to catch my breath and compose myself again.

Zack walked slowly, carefully balancing the hot cup as he set it on my desk. "How long do you think it will be before I get my big break, sir?"

I leaned over and ran my finger slowly over the curve of his ass. "That depends. You'll need some developing, some polishing, before you're ready for the big time. But stick with me. I'm the best there is."

"Yes, sir." He smiled sheepishly as he looked down at the floor. "I guess I do have a lot more to learn than I thought."

I took a long draw on the coffee. Then I put down my cup, got up, and walked over to the couch. "Show me your blowjob routine again. I'll give you a few pointers."

Two hours later, I knew I had a star. Zack got me hard again. He deep-throated me until my balls ached to come. He did one helluva strip tease. And when I bent him over the arm of the couch, he showed me he had the skills on which Backstage Casting built its reputation.

In the pornies, "special talent" refers to the "specialists" who can take the huge dicks and dildos. That's why my cock is so important. If an ass-pussy can take my tool, it can usually be trained to take the manmeat and toys that make audience assholes twitch with fear—and lust. Backstage provides bottoms who can—on demand—relax their asslips enough to take the really hung pornstars. Directors don't have to waste time with any more stretching and foreplay than the script calls for. They shout "spread," and a Backstage specialist winks his cute little pucker and takes a dildo or a plug or a cock the size of Montana straight up the wazoo. No bitching, no delays. That hole opens and the fucking starts on cue. Or the "talent" doesn't get paid.

Zack's pussy purred the minute I touched him. He wiggled and moaned, slutty enough to make any director slaver. I grabbed a glove and touched a lubed finger to him. His asslips kissed their way up my knuckles so fast I hardly saw them move.

"Good moves," I nodded appreciatively.

"Thank you, sir," he moaned. "Fuck, that feels good." He had a good growl. Lots of emotion. Good breathless overtones.

"You want more?" I laughed.

"Yes, sir!"

"Coming right up." Less than a minute later, I had four fingers in him and he was dancing on my hand. Real impressive hard-on, too. Lots of bottoms get soft when they're being stretched. Zack seemed to get harder.

"You're what, 8 inches?" I asked, wiggling my fingers, seeing if he could stay open. He did.

"Eight and 1/4, sir. When I'm fully erect." He moaned again. "Fuck, your fingers really feel good. If you want to open me more, that would be okay. Really."

I had to laugh. This one was definitely Backstage material. "That's as much as I can do without fisting you, which ain't my thing. You up for some toys?"

"Oh, fuck, yeah!" He pressed that cute little ass right back against my hand. "Plugs are cool, but I love dildos, man!"

The toys for the advanced auditions were in the credenza on the other side of the room. "Hold that thought," I said. I felt Zack's eyes watching me as I walked over and quickly grabbed an armful of implements in sterile bags: an assortment of plugs in gradually increasing sizes of extra large, several 10-12 inch dildos in various widths, and a vibrating prostate massager that would have made a horse proud. I dumped them on the coffee table next to a large bottle of gel lube and some towels.

"Pretty impressive, sir." Zack stayed bent over the couch, but he grinned and spread his legs even farther as I lined up my tools.

"We'll start with a plug." I picked up the smallest one, which was still a damn sight bigger than most human cocks. I figured Zack would probably tighten watching me. Anyone with a brain was going to clench his sphincter at the sight of something that size zeroing in for the kill. I slathered on lube, then touched the tip to his hole. "Open up, punk. Show me you can take it."

There was resistance, just for a second. Then fuck me if that cute little pucker didn't swallow the whole damn plug—all the way to the flange—in one long, slow, slide.

"Oh, fuck, sir!" Zack's arms were shaking against the couch.

"You okay?" I was impressed, but I was also concerned. Most people can't do what that young stud had done without feeling some serious pain.

"Shit, yeah! I just don't want to come yet. It seems like that would be kinda unprofessional, ya know?"

I couldn't believe it. I looked down, and one hard, hot, and very drippy stud-cock was waving over the cushions, a strand of precome drooling down like a huge wet spiderweb.

It was that way with all the toys. From Zack's reactions, I couldn't tell which ones he really liked best. Plugs, dildos—he seemed to love them all. He moaned and grunted and talked dirty enough to make any voiceover specialist lust after him. He leaned forward and ground his cock against the now towel-covered cushions. He arched his ass back at me as his pussy-hole swallowed progressively longer and wider toys, one right after the other.

I got him with the vibrating prostate massager though. He wasn't expecting that. I didn't turn it on until I'd worked it into him. It was so big that even with his talents, I had to go slowly. I could see by the way his cock jumped when I had the plastic bulge dead on his joyspot. I stroked his back, watching his muscles relax as he slowly dropped his head and groaned with pleasure at the stretch. Then, with no warning, I turned the vibrator on.

"FUUUUCCCKKKKK!!!!" I'd never heard a roar like that before. Zack's head shot up, his whole body stiffened, and his dick started gorping out come like his balls were draining themselves dry. He yelled and shook and spurted until I thought his bones would break. Oh, what a director would have paid for a come shot like that!

I cut the power as he collapsed forward. He lay face down, gasping, his body still quivering. He was way too tight for me to work the toy loose. So I waited until his breathing slowed before I slowly eased it out of him.

"I'm sorry, sir," he panted, whimpering into the upholstery as the tip pulled free.

"What the fuck for? Shit, I almost came watching you."

He wiggled his ass enticingly at me. I'd never seen anybody take that much and still want more. "But you didn't tell me to come yet!"

I shook my head, slowly working a condom over my dick. "I'll make an exception, since you're still in training and all. Now there's only one more part to the audition— if you think you can take it."

He slowly turned his head and looked over his shoulder, then his face broke into a huge grin. "I get to take your cock again, sir? Really? I mean, up my ass and all?"

This time I couldn't help laughing out loud as I slathered lube on my dick and slicked up his perfectly-loosened hole again. "Zack, I'm going to fuck you until your eyes cross, or at least until mine do. Now stick your ass back up here again." I slapped his butt sharply, smiling as he jumped.

When he didn't move, I stared down at him pointedly. "Zack?"

"Um, sir." His hesitation surprised me. He'd seemed to be game for anything. So I was really shocked when he blushed and grinned sheepishly at me. "This is kind of embarrassing, sir, but I get really snuggly after a come like that. Since this is an audition and all, I mean since there's no script I'd be screwing up, can I maybe lie on my back so I can see you while you fuck me? Maybe hug you a couple times? I'd really like that—if it's okay with you, of course."

This guy was one for the books. I was really starting to like him.

"Go for it, Zack. Just keep the towels under you. The couch only gets cleaned once a week."

"Yes, sir!" He grin was infectious. But he blew me out of the water when he turned onto his back on the damn couch and tipped all the way up onto his shoulders. His ass was the perfect height for fucking without my even having to bend over.

I slid in like a knife into warm butter. No resistance, just nice, smooth, open flesh kissing up my cock like a long, wet tongue job. I shivered as I sank in to the hilt. I didn't know that I'd ever felt an ass that receptive. Or one that I wanted so much. All of a sudden, I didn't care about the audition anymore. I wanted Zack just because I wanted him. I grabbed the back of his thighs and started a long, slow, sensuous fuck.

"You like that, pal?"

"Unh huh," he gasped. I looked down at his face and was surprised to see his eyes closed.

"I thought you wanted to watch."

"I do," he panted. "In a minute. I want to just feel for a second. Your cock is so big, sir, and you're fucking right over my prostate. Fuck, sir. It feels so good I don't know if I want to pee or come or pass out!"

He opened his eyes, and his baby blues sparkled up at me. I felt his smile all the way to my balls. He shivered as he watched me glide in and out a few times. "Do I get to watch you come, sir, or are you going to come up my ass?"

Hell, I had to know. "Which would you like?" I stroked in, sweet and slow.

He quivered and moaned, grinding against me. I slid in and out a couple more times. He felt so good, I had about made up my mind to just fuck his ass silly, when he blushed up at me. "I'd really like to watch your cock shoot. I didn't get to see before."

I laughed shakily, pulling out while I still could and throwing the rubber. "Pal, for a show like you've put on today, I'll be glad to let you watch."

I started to beat my meat, tugging down on my balls. I was close. Zack rolled over and fingered his hot little pussy, his eyes glued to my jerking fist.

"If you don't mind a suggestion, sir, a little ass stimulation can make a come even hotter. I can get you a little plug if you'd like. It'd make your prostate really happy."

There was still one unused plug sitting on the table—one of the more medium-sized of the extra larges. I nodded towards it. "Take it out of the wrapper, pal. And lube it up for me."

"Sir?" he asked. "Um, that's pretty big, sir. It's more my size. I'll be glad to get you another one."

"Lube it, stud," I growled. "Who the fuck do you think was Backstage's first star?!"

Zack looked at me in shock as I stopped jerking my dick long enough to grab a handful of gel and stuff it up my butt. Damn, my slicked fingers felt good sliding up inside me. My cock danced and drooled in response. It had been too damned long since I'd been fucked. I was looking forward to a good ass workout.

"Wow, sir!" Zack couldn't move fast enough as he slathered on the lube and held the toy out to me. "You mean, I get to watch you fuck a toy, too?"

"Even better." I turned around, grabbed ahold of the couch arm, and bent over. "You get to slide that sucker up my ass while I beat off. Now get busy, I'm about to come!"

"Yes, SIR!" I couldn't fault Zack's technique. He jumped right to my side, and he used a slow, firm, steady pressure as he worked that huge plug into my hungry hole. He had one arm around my waist, hugging me. Fuck, it felt good. I realized I really had gone too long without a good fuck up the ass—and without touching a man I cared for. Zack was giving me exactly what I needed. I groaned as he let go of the plug flange and I heard him turn on the vibrating prostate massager. I already knew what that kinky sucker was going to do. Sure, enough, a moment later, the huge buzzing toy touched the base of the monster plug up my ass. I groaned as the vibration traveled right up to my joyspot, just the way I was so hungry for. My ass clenched, like it was trying to pull in all the sensations surging into me. I stroked my shaft again, hard and fast, up and over the head— once, twice, three times. The spasms swept up from my guts to engulf me, and I was gone. I roared out my climax as my dick started spurting into my hand.

"Fuck, yeah, sir! Wow, man, you are hot!"

I shot till I thought I'd pass out. That fucker kept the vibrator on the base of the plug until I slapped his hand away. Then I fell over on the couch.

"Um, sir?" I heard the smirk, but I was too blissed out to care. "Did I pass the audition?"

"Yeah, you little shit." I kept my face in the cushion. I was too fucking tired to get up, and he was kissing my back, soft and sweet enough to make me shudder contentedly. "Be here at 7:00 Monday morning, stud. You're a Backstage man now."

Nice Work If You Can Get It

W. M. Williams

I'M RUNNING PATTIES OF GROUND-UP ANIMAL FLESH THROUGH THE broiler. It seems like half the campus is here. Must be green meatloaf night at the dorms. My sweat drips over the buns and I ignore it.

The assistant manager is just on the other side of the broiler from me. He wiggles and waves in the rising heat like bad TV reception but, even distorted, the guy is something to see. He's a few years older than I am—he's twenty-five, maybe twenty-six—but still smooth and clean-cut. I can't help staring; Rob is too pumped for his white button-down manager's shirt. Paint him green and piss him off and he'd come busting out like the Incredible Hulk.

He smiles right into my soul. He takes my hand and silently leads me away from the bustle of the kitchen, down the hallway narrowed by cartons of drink cups and plastic pickle buckets. No one notices, even though the dinner rush goes on.

He pulls me into the walk-in freezer. My breath clouds before me and goose flesh stands on my skin, but I can't break away from his penetrating blue eyes. He reaches for my belt, easing it free and popping the buttons of my greasy work pants with one deft motion. The cold rushes in, and my straining shaft arches before me in unreserved desire. Rob turns me and I offer no resistance, bending over a crate of frozen chicken nuggets and planting my feet wide for leverage on the icy floor. My stiffness throbs against a frosty box, and I tremble with anticipation. He tears open a packet of honey-mustard sauce and strong fingers lube my waiting hole.

"Jesus!" I cried as the vibrator popped through my anal ring. The shot of pain jerked me out of my fantasy for a moment, but it didn't take long for the buzzing phallus within me to once again become

Rob's thick, exciting length. I worked it deeper and the rhythmic sound of its mechanical purring, loud and brash in my bedroom, low and rumbling in the depths of me, became Rob's murmurs of passion. I coaxed my taut, swollen pole, squeezing harder, moving faster, relishing the surge of rapture inside me until, with a gasp, I buried the dildo its full eight inches and erupted with fountains of thick, hot spunk onto my own heaving chest. It was the best orgasm in weeks and I lay panting, still gripping my slackening organ, acutely aware of the rivulets of my juice as they trickled down my side and onto the bedclothes.

"I love how it feels the day after," I said. Carol and I walked along one of the sidewalks that criss-crossed the empty quad. "I can still feel the fullness, the movement in my body—almost as if something were still in me, still fucking me."

"Too bad you blew it with Rob," she said. "Now you'll never know if the real thing measures up to the dildo."

I shrugged. "He took me by surprise. I didn't even think he was gay."

"Get an eye exam, bud," she laughed, flipping honey-blonde bangs out of her eyes. "I've seen him check you out, along with every other cute guy who comes in."

I glanced over quickly at my petite friend. "Me? Cute?"

"Sure!" she said. "Hell, I'd jump your bones myself if I thought you'd get halfway into it. I've seen you in a Speedo, pal. You've got an ass that could crack walnuts and spit out the shells."

"What a ladylike remark!" I laughed. "Well, I'm glad all those workouts in high school tennis were worth something. I really only went out for the team so I could shower next to this one guy—whew, what a hunk!"

"I always sort of envied the lesbians in gym class," Carol said. "You know, for having something exciting to look forward to every day. I would look at the hottest cheerleaders, all sleek and wet with shampoo running down their breasts—I'd try real hard to get horny, but... "

"Hopelessly, desperately straight," I said, and she grinned and took my hand.

"This isn't high school anymore, Mark," she said, getting serious on me. "You can do more than peek in the showers and play with yourself. You've already squandered half of a four-year Golden Opportunity."

"I'm not exactly a virgin," I said.

"Standing in a toilet stall while some complete stranger sits on the pot and sucks your dick is hardly a fulfilling relationship."

"How do you know about stuff like that?"

"Oh, please," she said. "Everyone knows about the basement bathroom in the Media Arts building. It's, like, Homo Central."

I scowled. "Guess I'd better cross that tea room off the list."

"Why don't you cross them all off the list?" Carol stopped to face me where we still had some privacy, there being a clutch of people ahead. "Find a nice guy, have some fun, wake up next to the same person you were with the night before. I highly recommend morning sex, by the way."

"It's not that easy," I said. I wanted to look into her bright green eyes, but I couldn't.

"Sure it is," she countered. "You know you're gay, you've known it for years. You have to be who you are."

I looked at my feet and kicked a rock into the street. I had a sudden image of Beaver and Wally confessing to Ward about a broken window. I didn't like the feeling it brought with it.

"If you knew my mother—" I said softly. "She lost my Dad and half her marbles in the same accident. Her only child coming out of the closet would send her right over the edge."

"You don't give her enough credit, Marky-boy," Carol said. "She just might surprise you."

"We haven't had a conversation in six months that didn't involve a nice girl and grandchildren."

"You've spent your whole life leading her to believe that's what you want," she said. "Listen, it may take her some getting used to, but once she understands the truth she won't want you to live a lie. She'll want you to be happy."

I was not convinced, but it sure would be nice to drop the pretense.

"How did you know Rob was gay?" I asked.

"I put him to the test once." She grinned devilishly, as if recounting schoolgirl naughtiness. "I was wearing my red scoop-necked blouse, and you know that Marilyn Monroe thing, where you push the boobs together with your elbows and make the cleavage deeper than the Cumberland Gap? Rob never batted an eye."

I had to laugh. "Now I get it. Any guy who doesn't succumb to the beautiful Miss Carol Krupke must be gay!"

Her eyebrows went skyward. "Retract the claws, Miss Kitty! I'm just saying that guys usually check me out, and I notice it when they don't. Like, just about every guy's eyes will start out on my face, then slip straight down to my tits."

"Well, it doesn't matter now," I sighed. "He gave me my chance, asking me to that party, and I blew it."

"You can say that again," Carol said. "You could have gone to a great party and probably got laid, or at least you could have said, 'No thank you, Rob, but thanks for asking.' But what does Mr. Think-On-His-Feet do? Freaks out and makes a huge scene right in front of the whole crew. You're lucky you only got fired. Rob could have pulled you apart like a wishbone."

"Well, thanks for being so sympathetic."

"So what are you going to do?" she asked. "The new semester starts in three weeks."

"I don't know," I said, and I didn't. I'd thought about little else during my fruitless three-day job search. Quitting school would send Mom to the Happy Hunting Ground, I was sure, but nothing paid enough to make the five hundred I needed in three weeks. My tuition was covered by grants and loans, but dorm fees and books were up to me.

"You know what I'd do?" Carol sang like a child's rhyme.

"Yeah, but you're used to trading on your sexuality," I said, then yelped in pain when she gave me a solid shot to the arm. That girl had bony knuckles.

"What exactly does that mean?" she demanded, but her lips were curled at the corners as she fought off a grin.

"I just meant that women have always led men around by their dicks."

"Well, grab some foreskin and start tugging," she said. "It's the only chance you've got."

The hallway reeked of incense, the kind stoners use to cover up their dope in the dorm. I wondered if it was coming from Rob's apartment. There was no bell, so I knocked, softly at first, then in a crescendo of hammering as I overcame my own nervousness and the rock music pulsing inside. I was still pounding on the door when it burst open.

"What the fuck do you want?" Rob demanded. I thought the door would slam again before I could answer, but it didn't.

"I just had to tell you how sorry I am," I said, and it sounded pretty lame, even to me.

Rob regarded me warily. "You didn't come all the way over here just for that," he said.

"Well, no." I looked everywhere but his eyes. "Do I have to say the rest out here in the hallway?"

He considered, then waved me in and turned the stereo down a notch. It was a crappy little student apartment like hundreds in town, probably where Rob had lived since he was a junior or so. I didn't see an incense burner, and the odor was not as strong as in the hallway. It made sense—jocks aren't usually the stoner type.

"Actually," I said, trying to grin boyishly, "I came to beg you on bended knee for my job back." I hurried through an explanation of my financial straits and my sick mother, and as he listened his body language seemed to soften, which I took as a good sign.

"I swear I never meant to embarrass you like that, Rob," I pleaded with all the subtlety of a silent film queen. "It's just that you had me so turned on there was no blood left in my head. It was all in my dick!"

That didn't get a laugh, as I'd hoped, but it didn't get me tossed out the window, either. I settled for that.

"I couldn't believe you did that to me," Rob said, sounding more hurt than angry. "I thought you liked me."

"I do like you, Rob," I said. "God, if you knew how many times I've thought about you. Maybe we could pick up again from there—

you know, if I could just have my job back."

His eyes went cold. "I don't pay for sex," he said. "Either with money or with jobs."

"I didn't mean it like that," I protested, even while my heart pounded in the knowledge that I really had meant it exactly that way. Thanks a lot, Carol.

"I've already hired somebody anyway," he said, and started moving me toward the door with one big hand in the small of my back. "There are no openings."

"Now don't be too hasty," said an unfamiliar voice, and we both turned to look. A slim, handsome young man who was definitely not a weight lifter came out of what I presumed was the bedroom. He got my attention. "And who is our guest?" the dark-haired young man inquired, looking me over like he was judging Best of Breed.

"Mark Flannery," Rob said. "Used to work for me at Burger Barn."

"I'm Gregg Pemberton, with two g's," he said. Then, without a pause: "How old are you, Mark?"

"Twenty," I replied automatically. I was still young enough to be used to that question.

"Good, good," Gregg said, stepping around me and making no attempt to disguise his inspection of my body. "You need money?" he asked.

"Well, yeah," I said. "Five hundred bucks, by the start of the term."

"What if I said you could make five hundred dollars for a day's work?" Gregg smiled like a magician when you can't figure out his trick.

Rob looked at him as quizzically as I did. Suddenly something clicked, and I wasn't too pleased about it.

"Hey, I'm no hustler!" I snapped. I was a bit hypocritical, I guess, since two minutes earlier I had been perfectly willing to let Rob nail me to get my job back, but I rationalized that I had wanted Rob to nail me all along. Doing some fat old man for a few hundred bucks was a whole other thing.

"No, dear boy," Gregg chuckled. He was only a few years older than I, so 'dear boy' was a bit much. "Robert, don't you think young

Mark would be wonderful in our new video?"

"New video?" Rob said blankly, staring at Gregg for a beat before bursting into a huge grin. "Oh, that new video! Why yes, Gregg, I believe Mark would be perfect for the part of —uh—Chad."

"Chad!" Gregg exclaimed. "Why that's inspired! I was thinking Raoul—but, of course, you're right. He's the perfect Chad!"

"You two are making a video?" I asked suspiciously.

"Porno, darling," Gregg said. "The money flows like water. What do you think? A day of fucking and sucking gorgeous student hunks, and a cool five bills in your pocket?"

It took me a minute to wrap my brain around it. Porno? Me?

"I don't know, you guys," I finally said. "I don't think I could be up on screen like that."

"Why not?" Gregg demanded. "You're not ashamed of your body, are you? Trust me, you'd look fabulous in nothing but a smile."

"It's not that," I said, thinking of Carol and walnut shells.

"You are gay, aren't you?" It was like he was daring me to deny it.

"I'm gay all right," I said. "It's just that, I don't know if I can stand in front of a camera and tell the whole world that I am."

"He blames it on his sick mom," Rob sneered, "but he's really just a wimp."

I shot a look at him.

"He says it'd kill his mom, but I think he's just scared to deal with it," Rob said. "He'd rather quit school and spend his whole life peddling Barn Burgers than take a risk that somebody might call him a fag."

That hit me hard. There was no question that my mom would be truly upset to hear that her baby boy liked boy babes. But was that the only reason, or was I playing both sides of the street, putting off as long as possible any commitment in either direction? Was I trying to have my cock and eat it, too? Or was I really just a trembling little wimp cowering inside the status quo? How did Carol put it? You have to be who you are.

"Five hundred bucks—" I said slowly. "Cash money? Or with taxes and shit taken out?"

"You'd end up with five hundred clear," Gregg said.

"One day's work?"

"One day."

"Safe sex?"

"Absolutely. All cast members will be covered in the best latex."

I sure needed the bread. "OK, you've got a deal!" I announced, feeling instantly relieved that the decision was behind me and that I wouldn't have to quit school after all. My mom and my straight friends would never see a gay video in a million years, anyway.

Gregg held up his hand in the 'stop' gesture. "It's not quite that simple."

"It's not?"

"You need to pass the audition."

"Audition?" I croaked.

"Yeah," Rob said. "You don't think Spielberg just ups and hires some motherfucker, do you? Hell no! He does auditions and screen tests."

"You guys are not Spielberg," I said, a bit snidely.

"Nevertheless," Gregg said, "no audition, no video."

I thought a moment. My money problem had only been solved for ten seconds, but I had already gotten used to the idea. I wasn't ready to go back to being broke and on the verge of quitting school.

"When would this audition be?" I asked.

"No time like the present," Gregg said.

Aha, I thought. "And I suppose you guys will fill in for the other actors—sort of like stand-ins."

"What a great idea!" Gregg said, and shared a grin with his roommate.

Oh well, I thought. Did it really matter if I fucked eight guys or ten for my five hundred? I mean—once I'd decided to do it, the rest was mere detail.

I smiled and said: "Why not?"

The mood changed completely in the next seconds as all three of us grasped that the playful game of words was over and real, down-and-dirty sex was about to begin. Two pairs of eyes were stripping me and I felt like a goat staked out by lion hunters. I was also excited as hell. Part of my brain shouted: "Come on, lions!"

Gregg, of course, spoke first. "I think the first thing a producer needs is a good look at his star. Why don't you slip out of those clothes, Mark? Just remember, you're selling yourself!"

I wasn't sure how to start. I was used to fast, furtive sex at glory holes and in the dark corners of gay discos. So how would one do a strip tease? I self-consciously began to sway back and forth while I contemplated precisely what to do. My mind latched onto a song so old I'd never heard it anywhere but Classics 104, and had no idea who performed it.

"Slow dancin', swayin' to the music. Slow dancin', just me and my girl." It was perfect—except for the girl part.

Rob and Gregg watched intently as I eased my shirt over my head. I could feel their eyes on my body as I danced, sensed their growing excitement, and something began to change. They grinned at each other once or twice, but mostly their gazes remained locked on me. I slipped my jeans downward to reveal the jutting lump in my red bikini underwear, and Rob reached to adjust an answering lump in his own pants. I began to feel like the person in charge—the victor, not the victim. I was turning them on, drawing them in. They were mine for the taking, and they'd pay me five hundred bucks in the bargain.

"Jesus, what a body!" Gregg sighed. "Are you a swimmer?"

"Not in competition," I answered, undulating my red-clad fanny before them, never missing a beat. "I used to be a lifeguard, though."

Gregg massaged his crotch, which showed no lump that I could see. "I've always loved a swimmer's build," he mused.

I turned to face them fully, and my cock stuck out so stiffly that the waistband of my bikinis pulled away from my skin. Rob's eyes bulged.

"Oh, let's see that thing!" he muttered. He fell to his knees before me, reaching around to cup both cheeks of my ass in his huge hands and forcing me to continue my dance chiefly from the waist up. His eyes locked on my pulsing bulge, and I grinned in triumph. He looked to my face, beseeching. At my infinitesimal nod, Rob's powerful fingers skinned the bikinis down my legs and my rigid prick sprang forward to its full seven inches.

Rob never hesitated. Before my cock even stopped bouncing he was on it, his hungry lips engulfing my head and plunging down my shaft in desperate search of my pubes. His hot mouth was as powerful as the rest of him, and he pulled at my flesh with a suction I'd never felt before. Big hands kneaded my ass, and he crushed me to his face so forcefully I though he would pick me up and walk me around the room while he sucked. I had no doubt he could do it, too.

He pulled back and began to tongue my cock head, surprisingly gentle for such a bruiser. I opened my eyes—only then realizing they had been closed—and saw Gregg stepping out of his preppy slacks. His cock was very, very long, maybe ten inches, but thin enough I had no doubt I could touch my forefinger and thumb around it. Its head tapered off so sharply it practically came to a point, putting me in mind of a knitting needle with testicles.

"Whoa!" I cried as Rob really did lift me bodily, never taking his mouth off of me even as he deposited me on my back on the sofa. He engulfed me fully then, my cock stabbing into the slickness of his throat for a few precious seconds, then back to the heat and endless probing of his mouth and tongue. Gregg was suddenly there, looming his crotch over my face, and I caught the distinctive scent of Obsession For Men combined with pre-cum He aimed his long, slim stanchion to my lips as he lowered himself, and there was nothing to do but take it.

I didn't have to open wide, but there was lots of cock left when he reached gagging depth. I held his hips at the perfect distance, then worked that hot, hard pencil with my mouth and tongue, imitating the glorious things Rob was still doing to me. Gregg moaned loudly, and his hands clutched at the back of my head.

Rob lifted my legs over his shoulders, and in a second his probing tongue was across my balls and slithering into my cleft. I knew where he was going—I had willed him there if the truth were known—and I relaxed myself. It felt wonderful, that strong, slippery intruder making its way into my welcoming hole. In a moment my body responded on its own, opening, accepting, and I sighed in relief as Rob's stubby finger slipped in alongside his tongue and began to corkscrew into me. From nowhere there was cool, slick jelly, and the warmth of Rob's fingers soon turned me into a hot, slippery tunnel of anticipation.

In the next few seconds of delay I glimpsed a torn foil packet tossed onto the coffee table beside us, and then my legs were pulled firmly up and apart. The sofa creaked as Rob leaned in, and I felt his heat at my entrance. He was thicker than my dildo, thicker than anyone who had ever been inside me. A flash of fear raced through me, but it was tempered with tremendous excitement.

Rob began to ease his tool into me. I moaned in pleasure, for it was hot and hard and pulsing with a life no D-cell battery could ever duplicate. Then I felt his silken pubic bush nestle up against me and I knew he was fully in, and though I could see nothing but Gregg's belly I clearly pictured Rob's cock as not much longer than it was thick. I had the Abbott and Costello of cocks in me, one long and thin, the other short and fat, but I was in no danger of laughing.

"Are you OK, kid?" Rob grunted, holding himself tightly into me and gripping my thighs in his strong hands.

I made as positive a response as I could with a throat full of Gregg.

"OK, baby," he said, firming up his kneeling stance on the sofa. "Here we go."

Rob began to move: slowly at first, in short, one-inch stabs, but lengthening and speeding up until he was plowing into me at full depth. His balls felt huge as they slapped against me again and again. He thrust with such power that the whole couch rocked, forcing Gregg's cock too far into my throat and leaving me unable to protest.

It was a lucky thing Gregg decided to pull out when he did, because I was so short of oxygen the world was beginning to turn gray around the edges. I gulped air as he grabbed his long meat in a tight fist and flogged it, his nuts bouncing frantically before my eyes like the marionettes of an epileptic puppeteer.

Rob slammed into me harder than ever. I felt the slickness of our mingling sweat between us, savored the musky fragrance of sex that pervaded the room. Gregg's thighs tensed in my hands and his belly convulsed. Then with a grunt that didn't even sound human he began to spurt his seed. It sprayed my face and chest, three heavy gushes of it, and the bleach-white scent of semen filled my nose.

"Oh, Jesus!" Rob groaned, and thrust into me deeply. He held it there, all of him inside, his muscular frame flexing and shaking as he came. He pulled back and thrust twice more, then squeezed himself against me and trembled violently, panting like a winning triathlete. When he finally fell away the condom was distended like a balloon at the end of his short, thick cock; a latex golf ball on a tee.

They finished me off, double-teaming my body so expertly that I knew they were a long-term couple seriously into three-ways. Afterwards, I was a 160-pound wet noodle, and all I could manage was to lie there with eyes closed even after my chest's heaving slowed.

"I think he's asleep," I heard Rob say.

"He should be," Gregg said, "after the workout we gave him."

"He's got a great ass," Rob laughed softly. "Tight as a goddamn drum."

"He's one fine little cocksucker, too," Gregg added.

I enjoyed my eavesdropping, so I continued to play possum.

"I don't feel too good about what we did, though," Rob said, "letting him think he was going to make the money he needs. I mean, I was mad at him for embarrassing me at work, but Mark's always been a decent guy. I'd hate to see him get bounced out of school."

I tensed. I didn't like the idea of having been used so intimately. But, in another way, I did. I'd gotten my dream, and it was everything I'd imagined and then some.

"So give him his job back," Gregg said.

"I can't. After the shit I made up to justify firing him, the boss would never let me hire him back."

"Drag."

"Too bad we can't really make a video," Rob offered. "He'd be great in it."

There was a long silence. Gregg said: "Why can't we?"

"What the hell do we know about porn videos?"

"Well, we've watched enough of them," Gregg said, getting excited. "You know Curtis, that hunky black guy in Media Services? He makes tapes all the time with his friends, with music and special effects and everything. I've seen them and they're not bad. If we can just jack up the quality a little bit more, I'll bet we could sell them. And my cousin Marty works for a video distributor that handles porno. I'll bet he could get us in touch with the right people."

"We could round up enough guys," Rob mumbled, "but what do we do to pay them?"

"A piece of the action. A percentage."

"What about Mark's five hundred bucks?" Rob asked. "He needs that now."

"I'll pony up two-fifty if you do."

"I—uh—I guess I could," Rob said, glancing over at me sheepishly.

I didn't say anything. I just smiled. It hadn't even been a full day's work. I wondered if, maybe, we could extend the audition?

In Security

David Logan

I STOOD BEFORE THE OFFICE WINDOW AND SIGHED. THE SKY WAS BLUE and I could feel the sun's heat even through the glass. It was a perfect day to drop everything and hit the beach. Instead, I was stuck in this converted warehouse.

I turned back to face the small movie set beyond the door. Oh, well… That's what I was being paid to guard, not the great outdoors beyond the window. I stepped around the desk and moved quickly across the office. "Just put in your hours, man. It sure beats the hell out of flipping hamburgers," I mumbled to myself as I stepped out onto the set and shut the door behind me.

I moved around, doing what I figured I was supposed to. Larry hadn't been very specific when he hired me and still wasn't. "Just keep it quiet and don't let anybody in unless they're here for an interview," he'd said as he guided the blond out the door an hour ago. "I'll be back by two."

Larry was up from San Francisco to make a vid for his studio, and he wanted to use local talent. Some Oregon boy was going to be put on the map—maybe more than one, if Larry found the ten guys he was looking for. I figured he'd porked the shit out of the eight he'd already signed on—just from the sheepish look each of them gave me as he came out of the office. Of course, I'd heard their every moan and groan while they were bent over Larry's desk, too.

I plopped down on the couch that was part of the living room set and lay back against its cushions. It was sort of hard to imagine; next week naked guys were going to be sitting where I was now—making out, sucking, and fucking. Right now, it looked more like a furniture store, except for the tube of KY and box of rubbers beside the couch.

The door behind me opened, squeaking slightly. I jerked my head back over my shoulder as adrenaline pumped through me, even though I knew it was going to be just some kid looking for an easy thrill.

The most beautiful man in the world stood in the now-open doorway, looking around the set. He was tall, about six feet, with long black hair that was tied off into a ponytail, black eyes, and the typical features of an Asian. I remembered to breathe. My dick attacked my jeans in an effort to escape.

My jeans gave up after the first round—my meat was tenting my drawers on the first leg of its attempted flight to freedom. "I'm Corey," I said, blushing like a thirteen-year-old caught wacking-off.

He smiled and I melted. "Nice to meet you. My name's Shane. I'm here for an interview, or whatever it takes to get into this business."

"Larry's gone to lunch. He ought to be back in another hour and a half," I told him, my dick threatening to slip through the waistband of my shorts.

"Damn!" A frown touched the Asian's lips and quickly disappeared. "I knew I should have called ahead."

"You're welcome to hang out with me," I offered.

"Thanks. That'll save having to come back." He sat down on the other end of the sofa from me. "Are you one of the camera men?"

"Just security. They haven't started filming yet. Tell me about yourself," I suggested to break the ice.

"Well, I'm from a place five miles over the California/Oregon state line. I moved up here when I turned eighteen, a year ago. I've been going to college and had a good job, until the guy went out of business. I saw the ad for this in the local gay paper and decided to give it a try."

"Well, hope you make it," I told him. "I think you'd be great."

"Really?" Shane asked, turning to study me more closely.

"Sure. You've got great looks."

"Thanks! Now you—where are you from and all that other stuff?"

"I was from New York. I moved out here six years ago, when I was sixteen. Loved it here, so I stayed. I like being close to the beach.

And I'm trying to stay afloat until I get my degree next year."

Shane smiled again and it was a slower, warmer smile, sending shivers up and down my spine. He was *so* fine. "Do you really like what you see?" Shane asked.

"Yes," I admitted. "You're really—uh—sexy."

"What makes me so attractive to you?" he asked.

"Your being Asian does a lot for me, Shane. That makes you kind of mysterious. Something about you intrigues me a lot, something in your eyes just seems to pull me in and makes me want to get to know you more."

He thought about it for a minute. "I think that's so cool," he said finally. "Nobody's ever said that to me before."

I blushed and looked away, wondering if I had said too much.

"Want to see more of me?" Shane asked softly.

It was a question that made me look back in a hurry. Shane stood at his end of the couch, slowly stripping off his shirt. I gazed hungrily at the smooth torso as it became exposed. His nipples were the size of silver dollars, a bit flat, not real plump, and dark in color. His torso was deeply tanned, the muscles prominent, right down to the six-pack abs. I was speechless.

Shane smiled and dropped the shirt on the floor. He continued to strip, pulling his slacks off his legs and stepping out of them. He wore thong-style briefs, and I could see the outline of his package.

I reached out and touched the edge of the bulge. My finger traced the edge of the bulge as I became excited. I looked into Shane's face. He had his eyes closed, a smile on his face. My cockhead burrowed out of my briefs and found freedom.

"Feels good, Corey," he whispered.

I squeezed the swelling package inside the thong. Shane stepped forward, his hand finding my elbows and pulling me up to hug me to him. Our mouths found each other and we kissed.

"Can I undress you?" Shane murmured against my ear.

Shane's hands moved to possess my body, undressing me and freeing me from my jeans and tank top. "I love fur," he moaned, "and you've got so much of it." My pole sprang free and dripped its pleasure. He rubbed against me then, our abs grinding against each other's, our dicks dueling through our underwear.

I caressed the smooth, nearly-naked body pressed against mine, loving the feeling of his skin under my fingers. Shane moaned softly as my tongue found his. He ground his hips against mine, his clothed cock against mine—his fingers tweaking my nips as I too moaned my need.

I laid Shane down on the couch and pleasured his body with little kisses and licks from the hollow of his throat to the top of his thong underwear. I licked out his bellybutton and my lips moved back onto his chest to find first one nipple and then the other.

"Oh man!" he whimpered, his arms going around my neck to hold me against him.

"There's a lot more to come, Shane," I said as my fingers marched down his flanks until they reached his thong. My thumbs slipped inside the waist and began to ease it down onto his legs as I resumed sucking on his nipples.

Shane's fingers moved through the thick hair on my back like butterfly kisses.

My cock wanted this man's ass. To feel it flex around me as I plowed into him and have it grip at me as I retreated. I wanted to feel him come with me inside him, a part of his orgasm. But I held back, knowing that there was plenty of time to do that. Right now, I wanted to pleasure Shane, to take him right up as high as he could go until the only thing left was the ultimate release.

I skirted his freshly trimmed bush and his towering meat, diving for his balls, reveling in the glossy black of the hair and the scent of musk and jasmine I found there. "Oh, nice!" I mewled when my tongue touched his smooth, hairless balls. I sucked one of his eggs into my mouth and his ass came up off the couch.

"Oh, God! Corey!" he yelped.

I looked up at the wide-bodied tube with a helmet on top that flared even wider. My tongue began to move along the thick shaft toward that head. I was no longer thinking of fucking him and feeling his gut around my pole. I just wanted him to know all the pleasure I was able to give him, starting with my throat's manipulation of his cock. I reached the top and spread wide.

"Corey!" he cried. "It feels so damned good."

I began to suck harder, wanting only to please this man. I fluttered my tongue against his cock on the in-stroke and sucked hard on the out-stroke. Shane quickly reached his breaking point.

"Corey," he panted, looking down along his chest at me. "I want to be inside you."

I stopped sucking and reached for the tube of KY and box of rubbers. I worked a condom over his helmet and rolled it down his shaft. I squeezed lube onto Shane's cock. I stroked his cock and then worked the KY onto his latex-covered hard meat. "How do you want me?" I asked as I placed another glob of KY at my entrance.

"On your back," Shane answered as he sat up. "I want to be looking into those beautiful brown eyes of yours and feeling your forest on my fingers all the time, Corey."

I rolled onto my back. Shane stood over me, his cock standing straight out from him. He got onto the couch below me on his knees and lifted my legs onto his smooth chest. He then pointed his cock at my rose.

Shane slowly and carefully slid his seven inches into me. I moaned softly the whole time Shane entered me. Not from any pain but just the feeling of having mansex again and giving myself to the most beautiful man I'd ever seen. "You feel good inside of me," I told him as his pubes pressed against my low-hanging ballsac.

I felt great. I had a man's thick hardness inside of me and it was something I'd needed for too long. I smiled up at him. "Let's do it, babe," I told him, my hands finding each asscheek and pulling him hard against me. Shane started fucking me slowly, his cock reaching deeper into me with each long, slow stroke, possessing me as I'd never been possessed before. I looked up into his face and saw the most generous smile I'd ever seen on another man.

His wide helmet massaged my joy button with its every movement inside me. My dick returned to full erection as we settled into our coupling. I began to stroke it lazily as I gave myself up to what Shane was doing for me.

He bent over me, his tongue wetting my mat of hair before rearranging it to reach my left nipple. His lips pulled at the nub until it was hard enough for his teeth to bite. I jumped at the new stimulation, my whole body lifting off the couch. His tongue moved across my chest and did the same thing to my right nipple. Soon, his teeth were alternating from one to the other. His cock continued to move inside me in the same leisurely rhythm that he'd already established. My balls tightened and I started jacking myself in earnest.

I was past thinking. I was riding the waves of pleasure flowing over me from my ass and dick. I wanted the ride to go on forever. But my nuts were having none of it. They were riding the shaft of my hard cock.

Shane's face lifted from the forest of my chest and he smiled at me. "Give it to me, Corey. I want to feel you shoot your first load while I'm making love to you."

His lips touched mine then, his tongue pressing instantly between my teeth before I could even open them. I surrendered and shot my load, coating our bellies.

My cock stayed hard and my hands moved to the back of his head and held his mouth against mine. I felt the thin film of sweat that covered Shane's body. I possessed his mouth. My balls again rode my dickshaft. I had never had sex like this. A second orgasm was growing in me. It took me several moments to realize his movements had become faster. Shorter. His whole body was humping me hard. I felt his cock swell inside me. I exploded again. The spasms shooting through my gut grabbed Shane's cock. He shoved into me hard. A moment later, he collapsed on top of me, gasping for breath, his body spasming in after-shocks.

"Bravo!"

I concentrated on that one word. It hadn't been Shane who'd spoken. My eyes opened and I raised my head enough to see over the armrest.

Larry stood several feet behind me.

Turning red, I looked down at us. Shane's body covered mine, his cock was still deep inside me. I flamed crimson as I looked back at my boss.

He was grinning from ear to ear. "Looks like I've found the guys who'll give me a full crew... Wow! What an audition!"

"Larry..." I was pushing Shane off me and sliding up the cushion to get his dick out of me. "Sir, I didn't mean..." I glanced back at Shane. "It just sort of happened."

"Jesus! Don't apologize, Corey. You two are hot. I mean H O T! I've got a couple of contracts in the office if you'll sign them."

Shane sat up and looked at Larry. "You mean that you want us—Corey and me—to be in this movie of yours?"

Larry snorted. "I mean, you two are going to be fucking stars. In this picture and a lot of others as well."

Shane smiled at me. "You'll probably make better money than you do now, Corey."

"Yeah," I mumbled and studied for a few moments more the most beautiful man I'd ever seen, "but will I have you?"

His smile widened, taking over his whole face. "I think I can handle coming home to you."

In Search Of...

Vic Howell

I FELT SOMEONE'S EYES GLUED TO MY BACK AND I STIFFENED. IT WAS the damned guy who'd been everywhere I was this past week. Watching me. Didn't the son of a bitch have a fucking life?

I forced myself to relax. I turned and quickly laid twenty-four beef patties down on the grill and watched them sizzle like hell as they unfroze. I didn't look up but managed to survey the dining room beyond the counter.

Yep! It was him all right. Standing there against the condiments station, watching me. Like he didn't have anything else in the world to do but watch me. I automatically flipped each row of four patties and glanced over to see if the buns were ready.

I'd been flipping hamburgers the past six months. I could do it in my sleep. In fact, I had done it in my sleep—cooking had become a staple for my nightmares. Hamburger patties rolling after me, uncooked and dripping blood and grease—like that crazy classic movie about killer tomatoes.

I went on autopilot and allowed myself to wonder why the guy had decided to key on me. I wondered if he was from the parole board. But why? I was clean. I reported every two weeks and pissed for them every month. Outside of not accepting his regular invitations to go to church, I did anything my parole officer even remotely suggested.

I tried out vice cop on the guy. His little cop manual would have told him criminals repeat themselves almost fifty percent of the time. Ergo, Jesse Hays was probably selling drugs again. Go bust him and get a feather in your cap. Only, the bastard hadn't hit on me for anything smokeable or eatable yet and this shit had been going for the better part of a week.

The guy was about my height and weight but had long, shoulder-length black hair. No small-town cop would ever do that; it wasn't macho enough for them. He was also wearing a stud in his ear. That definitely took him out of the cop and parole board category. The only other thing I could think of was he wanted a shot at my bone.

It wasn't like I wore a big Q branded on my chest or something. Shit! I wasn't even queer. I just didn't have a girlfriend—who could, on the wage I made? If I worked enough hours to have decent money, I didn't have the energy—even if I could find a nice girl at four o'clock in the morning which was when I got off. I closed Evansdale's Hamburger Heaven six nights a week and was finally making six dollars an hour—taking home a little more than two hundred a week after taxes.

Another two months working sixty-hour weeks (thirty-nine of them on the clock) and I could get out of the old man's house and afford a clunker. I'd gone a year and a half without seeing a girl while I was a guest of the Iowa Correctional System; another year without one wasn't going to kill me. Besides, I was only twenty. I had the rest of my life in front of me.

And I sure as shit wasn't going to fuck it up again. That year and a half in the slammer convinced me good that drugs and everything else the people of Iowa didn't like were not for me. I was straight-arrow all the way, even down to sporting a buzz cut.

I didn't look bad. Six feet, blond hair, and 180 pounds, I kept well-toned while I was in prison. It was either spend hours at the gym or be somebody's pincushion—somebody with a gut and connections that gave him leverage. It wasn't that I had a hate on for gays. I lived and let live. It was just that I couldn't see me spreading my legs and taking a big one up the butt. It just wasn't the way the old man had raised me.

The guy watching me didn't look especially faggoty. It was just that he kept watching me and that was the only reason I could think of that made sense—him being gay. There had been enough all-guy guys in prison who oohed and ahhed the moment they got a dick up their asses that I knew a man didn't have to look like Liberace to be a little funny.

Birds tweeted sleepily to each other as I locked up Hamburger Heaven and started to walk home. The cool autumn breeze chilled the sweat that covered me from stripping the floors. Evansdale was peaceful at four in the morning, there wasn't even a cop in sight.

I crossed the street and entered the park making straight for the only home I'd known in my twenty years. I pulled up my shirt hem to wipe my face.

"Yo, Jesse Hays!"

The unexpected voice caught me and spun me around, my heart pounding in sudden fear. I couldn't see anybody, just the trees closing in menacingly on the path I walked twice a day, six days a week. "Who's there?" I asked and wished my voice hadn't broke.

I saw movement under an old elm beside me and a figure started out from under the branches toward me.

"I'm about to become your very best friend, Jesse," the guy chuckled. "The name's Doug."

I could finally make him out as he entered the moonlight. It was the guy who'd been my shadow the past week. "Bullshit!" I growled softly. "Why've you been following me around?" I demanded, raising my voice so it would reach him.

"Checking you out," he answered and stopped a couple of feet from me, grinning back at me.

"What are you, gay?" I growled, still trying to swallow my heart and praying that it would work again like it was supposed to. I wasn't ready to die in Evansdale Park.

"Maybe."

"Great!" I groaned. "Just the fuck what I need—some queer asshole stalking me."

"Just how much do you bring home every week, Jesse?"

I stared at him. What was he going to do, pay me to let him give me a blowjob? "More than you can talk about," I told him and started to step away.

"How about two bills for an hour's work?" he asked, ignoring my rejection. "Cash?"

That stopped me fast. In mid-step. Two hundred, free and clear? I turned back to face him; he had my complete attention. I'd even go along with some sex stuff for that kind of money. "Where's this going?" I asked.

Doug grinned, reading me and knowing he'd broken through to me. "I'm in room 315 of the Evansdale Inn, in the back. Why don't you meet me there—say, at two this afternoon? That ought to give you time to get some sleep—get cleaned up, too."

"What're we going to do there?"

He chuckled. "We're going to have a serious talk. Then, and only then—if you like what I've got to say—you'll get to earn your two bills. There's a whole lot more where that comes from, too. Does that sound okay to you?"

"We're just going to talk?" I asked suspiciously. He nodded. "You won't try any funny shit unless I want to get into it?"

"You are a suspicious one, Jesse—but I guess prison can do that to a guy—"

"How did you know about me being an ex-con?"

He smiled. I decided he had a real cute smile and that sort of shocked me. "Will you be there at two this afternoon?"

I nodded.

My heart was in my throat at two-to-five that afternoon when I knocked at his door. I guessed there was sex in the offering once I was in the room, but hadn't yet figured out how far I was willing to go with it. I had to admit, though, I was kind of curious. A hell of a lot more curious than I'd ever been in prison. I'd woken up realizing I was real fucking horny.

"Hi, Jesse," he said opening the door wide. "Come on in."

I took two steps forward and stopped while he shut the door behind me. I looked around the room and saw it was pretty much standard-issue motel fare, same as back when the old man let me travel with him sometimes. Doug's fingers brushed my hand and lingered a couple of heartbeats too long. I flinched.

"So, Doug, how am I supposed to make this two hundred dollars you suggested very early this morning in the park?"

"Want a beer?" He crossed the room to an ice chest I'd not seen earlier.

"Soft drink if you have it. I need caffeine more than I do alcohol this early."

He chuckled and pulled out a can.

"Why have you been following me around?" I asked as he returned to stand in front of me. "And what's this about two bills?"

"Serious talk first, remember? Take the bed and get comfortable." I studied him and he laughed. "We're going to talk first, Jesse. Just promise me that you'll keep an open mind and that you'll hear me out."

"Sure. Why not?" I said flippantly and detoured around him to the bed. "Draw me a real pretty picture." I opened my soda, took a long swallow, plopped down on the bed, and waited.

"The long and short of it is I'm a talent scout, Jesse." He propped his ass against the tiny desk beside the room's television set and faced me.

"You're a talent scout? They pay you to shadow a guy a week at a time? To get up the shit on him? Come on, Doug—or whatever your real name is—that sounds a lot more like a private eye than it does a talent scout."

"It does, doesn't it?" he chuckled. "Okay, add in the fact that I'm gay. That the talent I scout for is for gay vids. And that I find you one fine looking piece of manmeat. I just went a little overboard, that's all."

So, here it was. Out in the open. He was gay. He liked what he saw when he saw me. I wasn't mad, but I still didn't know how it was going to go. "More than a little," I admitted. "I didn't know whether to shit, have a heartattack, or come out fighting all this past week. There aren't many people who like to get stalked."

He hung his head like a little kid. I knew right then there was no way I was getting mad at him. There wasn't any use; he was the sort of person a guy couldn't stay mad at long enough to make it worthwhile. "I did get carried away," he mumbled. "I'm really sorry about that."

"How about this money—two hundred for an hour, you said?"

"For a screen test."

"Screen test?"

"I find talent for the biggest studios in California—and they're always looking." He looked down at his hands. "I also manage the guys I get into the business."

"Manage?"

"Set up their appearances, get them into the best paying films—" He snorted. "Doug Yorston, everybody's favorite mother hen."

"And you want to play mother hen to me?"

He grinned impishly. "That wasn't exactly what I had in mind, Jesse Hays."

Uh-oh. Here it came. Which way to play it? I could really use a couple extra hundred. I was horny and had been that way much too long. And this Doug Yorston was a good looking guy. I wouldn't have any problem letting him have at my bone, even for free.

"This screen test—where would you conduct it?"

He looked up, his face showing his surprise. "Here, of course."

"I don't see anything that looks like lights or cameras."

"I've got a camcorder. It takes only a few minutes to hook it and set it up on remote."

"So, I do this screen test with you?" He nodded. "And exactly what am I supposed to do in this screen test?"

"Just the usual—" I waited. A few moments later he gave up and got specific. "You get sucked, you fuck, you suck, you get fucked."

I sat up straight, making damned sure my feet were firmly on the floor. I wasn't ready for very much of this bullshit. "Let me get this straight, pal," I growled. "You want me to get poked in the mouth and ass and, if I do, you'll pay me two hundred dollars?"

He laughed and stood up. "If that's the way it looks on camera I wouldn't even send the cassette on."

"Huh?"

"A screen test is to see how hot you look on camera. How easy it's gonna be for the folks out here in the cornfields to turn on to you—"

"You're talking about me sucking dick."

"You're getting two bills for it, too."

He had me on that one. I quickly decided I could maybe go along with him that far. It depended on how right things felt as they were going along. "And taking one up my ass," I voiced my major concern.

Doug chuckled. "If you get into this business, sooner or later you're going to do it."

"Maybe so. But I'd be getting paid a lot more than two hundred dollars for it."

"That's true." He pursed his lips thinking about it. "Tell you what. We'll be sporting about it. Whoever has the longest dick does top."

"Between you and me?" He nodded. I looked at him closely. He was two, three inches shorter than my six feet and maybe twenty pounds lighter. For the first time in my life I studied another guy's crotch and found myself wanting to see his porker. As close as I could tell we were pretty evenly matched. Only, I had seven and a half inches in my jeans and knew that was a lot bigger than average. I had a better than even chance of fucking butt today. Either way, I got two hundred dollars.

"I'll take you up on it, pal; only, you'd better have lots of lube because you're gonna need it." He shrugged. "How about the money? Put it on the table so I can see it."

I watched him move silently to the little table by the window, pull out his wallet, count out four fifties, and put them in the center of the table. He turned to face me and smiled again. He stepped to the closet and pulled out a traveling case. Unzipping it, he said: "the action stays as close to the center of the bed as we both can keep it—that's where this thing is going to be aimed."

I nodded slowly, in shock at how far I was letting this thing go. I had to be fucking crazy to suck dick or even think of one popping my butt. I looked at Doug and relaxed as I let myself study him. He had a nicely shaped ass. I was going to like digging into that. He was pretty good looking too. I could enjoy the afternoon and walk away from it, two hundred dollars richer.

"How do you want to play it?" I asked, comfortably cocky again. I even smiled as he lined the camcorder up on me.

He grinned back at me as he flicked the thing on. "Why don't you strip for the camera, Jesse. Just make it sexy for us."

I looked at the dark, round eye of the camcorder for a moment and something clicked inside my head. I wanted to turn Doug on, him and the people who would see this cassette. I smiled and realized that I was a closet exhibitionist stepping out of the closet for the first time. I wanted to do a smack-up job. And I wanted Doug to get hot seeing me get out of my clothes. I wanted him begging for it before I gave it to him.

I toed my sneakers off and stood. I smiled at the camera, licking my lips with just the tip of my tongue, and began to sway ever so slightly. I unsnapped the waist button of my jeans and began to ease my t-shirt out of them.

Easing into a bump and grind, I began to move the shirt up over my hard six-pack and onto my chest. I kept my eyes on the camera and didn't let a thought in my head. The shirt passed over my head and I threw it back on the bed. My fingers worked the zipper down my jeans and I turned up the heat of the bump and grind as I spread the flaps and began to ease the denim back and forth over my groin.

I wasn't wearing underpants, I never did—except for when I was in prison. Instinct kept me slipping my opened jeans across my front and showing just my pubes to the camera. "Turn around now," Doug told me, "and slip them on off. When you're completely naked turn back around for the camera. Just wiggle that butt while you're mooning me."

I swung around, bent over the bed, and ground my ass wantonly. Standing back up, I slipped the denim over my asscheeks and down onto my thighs. I buried my face in the bedcovers and wiggled my now naked butt for the camera and Doug to see as I slipped my jeans down to my ankles. I toed them off and was naked.

I was harder than I could remember ever being. I stood up, swung around, and, gripping my big dick at the base, pointed it at the camera. I was still bumping and grinding when Doug's fingers encircled my meat. I let go of my pole, putting my hand on his bare shoulders to support myself, and began to hump his hand.

"Nice, Jesse," he said against my ear before he began to nibble at my lobe, the fingers of his other hand spreading across my ass cheeks. His lips traced my jaw out to my chin. I felt his cockhead poking my bellybutton.

I looked down at what he had. I reached down between us and took both of them and brought them together. He was poking my pubic bone and I couldn't even feel his pubes tickling my helmet. He had me by a good inch. I closed my eyes and groaned.

I was sweating. I was hornier than I'd ever been. I didn't know what I was doing; I was flying on instinct. I kissed him, my hands coming up to the back of his head to hold his face against mine. My hard cock pressed against his naked stomach, against his meat. He moved closer, his tongue slipping between my teeth as his groin pressed against mine. Our cocks, trapped between us as we began to grind against each other, began to leak.

Doug broke the kiss, his lips moving over my chin to my adam's apple and then to the hollow of my neck. His fingers traveled down my spine from my shoulders to my asscheeks. I stretched in hunger, a hunger I'd never expected or known before. One more intense than I'd ever known with a girl.

His lips found one of my nipples. His teeth bit it gently and I groaned as pleasure shot through my body. My dick got harder and I knew it was going to split the skin encasing it. He brought one hand up from my ass and its thumb and forefinger began to tweak my other nub. I ground against him, wanting him. Wanting the pleasure he was giving me to go on forever.

He moved me until I was lying on the bed. His lips slid from my nipples rapidly down to my pubes to climb my pole. I was panting, my body overloaded in sensations. I reached out and took his dick, my fingers forming a fist around it. He straddled me and I watched with fascination as his tool came closer and closer to my face.

His tongue washed my helmet and I was beyond thought. My hard meat moved into his mouth and penetrated his throat. I felt his lips press against my pubes. He swallowed to massage my knob again and again. I shuddered and bucked at the unfamiliar stimulation.

His cockhead, leaking pre-cum, pressed against my lips and I opened them to take him into my mouth, my hands moving instinctively to knead his asscheeks and direct him. Doug Yorston began to hump my face, and I gagged when his helmet pushed against my virgin tonsils the first time. It was but a momentary distraction, however, and could not pull me away from the storm growing in my balls. I took his meat into my throat with his next thrust.

His fingers found my cleft and I spread my legs to give him easier access. He quickly raised one of my legs and then the other to put them under his arms. I was hiked and exposed, my mouth and throat full of cock, as he continued to suck my meat and his finger made increasingly smaller circles around my back entrance. Sensation after sensation crashed over me, numbing me to anything but the pleasure pulsing through my body.

My balls tightened against my root as Doug continued to deep-throat me. His spittle seeped down to join his finger at my pucker. I was bucking in anticipation of my approaching orgasm. He shoved his finger through my assmuscle and I groaned around the thick shaft of his cock as all of it slipped into my throat, my nose buried in his balls.

I erupted. His finger found my joy spot and I blew everything my balls ever thought of producing. A second finger joined the first inside my ass and I gave him another rope from somewhere. A third joined the other two and my sphincter didn't even resist, I was so spent.

I lay staring up at his thighs, at his balls spread across the bridge of my nose, trying to breathe and finding out I couldn't. His cock sealed my air passage. I pushed at his hips with the little strength I still had.

He fell to my side, pulling his cock from my throat. I gasped before I did anything, filling my lungs with air. He was still licking his lips when I looked over at him, his head resting on my thigh. He grinned.

"Tell me you didn't like that, Jesse," he dared me.

I glanced down at my softening and glistening meat and knew I couldn't. It had been the best sex I'd ever had. I didn't look back at him; I just stared at my dick and tried to imagine the life the damned thing seemed hellbent on manufacturing for me.

"One more thing left in this screen test, Jesse. You want to take my word for it or do you want to measure them?"

"Word for it?"

"As to which of us is bigger. I'll tell you right now that I am."

He wiggled his fingers and my eyes bulged at the sensations that caused in my butt. My dick decided to climb back into erection. "That felt good," I mumbled to my surprise.

"What comes next will feel even better, Jesse."

"I'm not sure about this—" I said, starting to backtrack.

Doug pulled his fingers out of me and pushed himself off the bed. He went to his bag, pulled out a condom, and tore it open. I was in shock how empty I felt without his fingers in me—I actually felt barren.

Picking up a tube of KY, he returned to me. He stood beside the bed and held the rubber out to me. "Put it on for me, Jesse. For both of us."

My dick was hard and I knew I wanted to feel his again. Feel him again—all of him—but especially his meat. I sighed and held out my hand. I turned to face him and spread the pancake of latex over the crown of his pole. I rolled it down onto the shaft slowly, marvelling at how big and how hard he was.

He handed me the tube of lubricant. "Put some of this onto the head of my dick, Jesse. Rub it all around and get it slippery."

I squeezed gel out and worked it onto the condom's skin. I couldn't take my eyes off his meat. How it jutted straight out in front of him. How wide it was—especially the helmet. I wondered how something as big as that could get into me.

"Lie down, Jesse." Doug's voice was soothing, relaxing. "We're both going to be feeling good in a few."

I lay back and he crawled onto the bed, lifting my nearest leg to pass beneath it. "Go real slow," I told him, surrendering to my curiosity and my growing desire. "I've never done this before."

He squeezed gel on the tip of two of his fingers as he situated himself between my splayed legs. I felt the cool stuff touch my ass-lips but neither finger stopped there. My eyes bulged as they continued to enter me. My dick drooped at the shock.

"Rest your legs up on my chest," Doug said as he twisted his fingers inside me.

My pole seeped pre-cum and jumped back to its erection. "Jesus!" I mewled as I hiked my legs and laid them on his chest. I was consciously starting to wonder what his dick would do to me if just his fingers could get me hard and oozing.

His cock pressed against his fingers in my hole but it was at a difficult angle. "Cross your ankles behind my head, Jesse," he told me. "That'll raise you up to the right height."

I did as he suggested and he moved his free hand up to my hip. "You aren't going into me with your fingers still there, are you?" I groaned as I gazed down my body, past my hard pole lying on my stomach, at his abs tensing just beyond the back of my legs. He spread his fingers inside me wide.

Pressure increased at my pucker. Just as I was about to pull away from it, his fingers pulled out of me. Before I could even think of shutting my back door, the head of his dick was past my assmuscle. His other hand came up to my free hip and held me steady.

Doug smiled down at me. "Want it slow and in stages—or all of it fast?"

I felt full and that made me uncomfortable—but I didn't hurt. "Give me all of it," I told him.

He nodded, his smile becoming a grin, and humped his hips hard at my bottom.

I fought back a scream. My virgin chute was stretched wider than it'd ever been before. My cock drooped until the helmet of his dick massaged my nut as it pushed over and past it. My meat drooled and tried to reach another erection but he was pushing deeper into me by the second, stretching me and shocking my body. Inch after inch pushed into me until I felt his balls spread against my asscheeks and his pubes scratching my ballsac.

"I'm in," he announced.

"Thank god!" I moaned.

"Grind your butt around on my dick, Jesse. Hump it like you would do a dildo."

A dildo? Shit! I wasn't a fucking woman. Then I realized what was buried in my ass. I chuckled.

Doug gazed down at me quizically. "You all right?"

"You're fucking me," I giggled.

"Grind that ass for us, Jesse."

I did. Rotating and humping. Alternating and at the same time. His cock stayed buried in me. My pole got so hard it threatened to burst the skin. I started stroking my meat in no particular rhythm— just getting deeper into the feeling rushing over me.

I didn't know when he started to fuck me. My eyes were shut and my head was rolling from side to side, my mouth open. I made noises that were more grunts than words. My body jerked as wave after wave of new sensations crashed over me, each better than the one before.

I was aware of Doug leaning into me, against my legs. I was aware of the movement of his cock through my body. I was and I wasn't. I was alone. I rode killer waves and climbed the highest mountains. I walked on the stars. Mountains rose under my feet and became volcanos spewing lava across my chest, onto my face. And I continued to ride and be ridden at the same time.

I was gasping for breath and felt numb all over, beyond death and far into the depths of life. Somehow, I forced my eyes to open to find Doug lying on top of me, his lips pressed against mine, his tongue feeling my tonsils.

He rose up on his elbows to smile down at me. "You are a natural, Jesse Hays."

"Yeah?"

"You shot three loads before I came—the last two without even touching yourself."

I wiggled under him and felt my cock hard against his abs. "You still hard?" I asked.

"You want another round?"

I grinned up at him. "Yeah!"

He chuckled. "Before or after we talk about your future in the adult film industry?"

"Fuck me. Then I'll worry about doing a vid."

He pushed himself up on his knees. I kept my legs with him so he didn't pull out. "You're going to have to get your parole transferred to California, Jesse," he said after we were lined up and comfortable.

"Why?" I mumbled as he pushed all of himself into me.

"So you can live with me."

He didn't let me answer that one before he was pounding his cock in and out of my ass. The way I was feeling right then, it sounded like the brightest idea since man first stood on two legs. I bucked up to meet his thrusts.

Type Casting

Michael Stamp

CASTING CALL. CATTLE CALL IS A MORE APT DESCRIPTION. HUN-dreds of pornstar wannabes in one place, each with a stiff cock in his pants and dreams of fame and fortune in his head. Most directors refuse to audition that way, but me—I love it. There's something about walking into a room full of hot, horny men that always gets my blood pumping and my cock jumping.

I've learned the world is full of good-looking men, and very few of them are actors. But there are plenty of other men who'd love to fuck in front of a camera, so every couple of months I hold an open audition, hoping somewhere in the crowd will be that special man, the one who countless gay men will jerk off to while they watch him on their TV screens. It hasn't happened so far, but I've always been an optimist.

My ad in the trades is always discreet. I list only the time and place of the audition, and my company name. I don't need to spell out what the audition is for, or even the "type" I'm looking for. Anyone who knows Hard Epic Videos knows what kinds of parts I'll be casting, and that hot, July morning, the reception area of my Los Angeles office was packed with a horde of tantalizing manflesh of all ages, shapes and sizes. I've been doing this for 25 years, but each time is like the first time, with me feeling like a kid in a candy store.

Hard Epic is a one-man show, and I'm that man. I keep control of every aspect of the company because I built it from nothing. I'm the writer, producer, director. Hell, I've even been on screen. Money was so tight back when I first started the company that I had to act in some of the early videos myself. If you ever come across any vintage Hard Epic videos, look for an actor named Kenny Mack. He won't be hard to spot. Just look for a 6'4" redhead with ten inches of thick, uncut cock. The red hair may be flecked with white now, but those ten inches are as impressive now as they were then.

I stood by my office door, surveying the hopefuls. There were at least a dozen muscle studs in posing straps, all with pumped-up pecs, 16-inch biceps, and thighs like tree-trunks. Then there was the contingent of clones, with flashing white teeth and perfectly-coifed hair, most of them dressed in obscenely-tight lycra bicycle shorts and tank tops cut off to expose the washboard abs they spent at least two hours a day at the gym crunching.

The crowd was mostly early- to mid-twenties, but I did spy a few kids who looked so young I knew I'd have to check their ID's before the audition went any further. I don't work with underage kids. There's a market for them, but dealing with the law is just too much of a hassle, so I make sure all my actors are legal. One man in the crowd caught my eye, but not because I thought he'd be perfect for my next film. What made him stand out were his clothes.

Like I said, most men know what I'm looking for and come dressed for the part, or at least they wear something that really shows off the merchandise. But not this guy. He was dressed in a gray three-piece suit so baggy it was impossible to tell what kind of a body he had. His dark brown hair was slicked back, either from the heat or hair gel, I couldn't tell which. And he was wearing wingtips. He was early twenties, and I thought he might not have been a bad-looking kid if it weren't for the thick, black, horn-rimmed glasses he was wearing. He'd brought a briefcase with him, and in his shirt pocket was the ultimate geek accessory—a pocket protector.

I tried to remember. Had my accountant told me he was sending someone over to look at the books today? No, I would have remembered that. Was it possible the guy was here to audition?

I glanced at my receptionist, Peter, and raised my eyebrows as if to ask, "How did he get in here?" Peter only shrugged his shoulders and rolled his eyes. I had to laugh. Peter's a good kid. The receptionist job doesn't pay that much, but Peter can tell you, the perks are great. Enough hot men pass through my doors every day to fuel Peter's fantasies, so he doesn't mind trading off ogling the merchandise in exchange for a little less in his paycheck.

I felt sorry for the geek, sitting there among some of the best-looking men in LA, and hoping to save him from being humiliated, I went over to him and said: "I have a feeling you're in the wrong place."

"Isn't this the open audition for Hard Epic?" he asked anxiously.

So he wasn't in the wrong place. Which made his being here even worse. "Yes it is," I said, "but I'm afraid you're not what we're looking for."

"How do you know?" he asked.

"I know," I assured him. "I'm Angus MacKenna."

It was obvious he recognized my name. "Look," he said apologetically, "I didn't find out about the audition until I'd already left for work this morning, so I didn't get a chance to change before I came."

"I don't think that would have made any difference."

"Please, Mr. MacKenna, you have to give me a chance," he insisted.

"I don't have to do anything," I told him.

"But I deserve the same chance to be considered as everyone else here—"

The kid was starting to annoy me, so I cut him off angrily. "Look, kid, the only thing I'd consider you for is a porn version of *Revenge Of The Nerds*, and since Hard Epic won't be making that particular video any time in the near future, I wouldn't want you to waste your time."

There was a roar of good-natured laughter from the men around him. A few of the clones clucked sympathetically in his direction. His face reddened in embarrassment but, to his credit, the kid didn't turn away. He was only about 5' 7", but he pulled himself up to his full height and looked me straight in the eye. "Well, Mr. MacKenna, it's my time—so, if you don't mind, I'll wait."

"Suit yourself," I shrugged, then ordered the rest of the men to follow Peter down to the sound stage.

I started out by testing men in pairs of my choosing, just to see how they looked together. Hard Epic fans like the traditional—big guys, hung like horses, sticking their massive cocks up the asses of smaller guys. So I started pairing up the muscle studs with clones, then with some of the real young-looking guys. Nothing worked. Most of the muscle guys were big—so big that when they started fucking, the guys underneath them disappeared. Seeing a top's cock sliding in and out of a hungry hole is a favorite scene in all my videos, but with these guys, whatever angle we tried, their bulk obscured the come shot, the kiss of death in porn videos.

About an hour into the tryouts, I remembered a long-distance call I was expecting from a distributor. I was going to tell Peter to go up, take the call, and make my apologies, but he was having such a great time hanging out with the actors that I decided to let him enjoy himself and went up to wait for the call myself.

The nerd in the suit was still in the reception area when I got back. I had hoped he'd given up and gone to his real job—but there he was, still sitting in one of the overstuffed armchairs. I said nothing to him, and went into my office. It was a short call. The distributor and I came to an arrangement we were both happy with, and five minutes later I was ready to head back downstairs. When I opened my door, I almost fell over the kid. "For Christ's sake!" I growled, struggling to keep my balance.

"I'm sorry, Mr. MacKenna," he apologized. "I just thought you might have changed your mind about letting me audition."

I was going to call security and have him thrown out of the building. Then I had a better idea, one that I was sure would discourage him more than any hired muscle could. "Okay, kid, you win. You want an audition, you got one."

"That's wonderful, sir. You won't be disappointed, I promise you."

He turned and started to head out to the elevator, but I stopped him. "Wrong direction," I said. He looked momentarily confused, then it began to dawn on him where his audition would take place. "That's right, kid. This is going to be a private audition, so if you have a problem with that—"

I could see his mind working as he ran the possible scenarios in his head. Was this a legitimate offer? Or was I just going to humiliate him by fucking him and then sending him on his way? I thought sure he'd decide I was playing him for a fool and leave, but instead he said, "No problem, Mr. MacKenna. No problem at all."

"Fine. Go into my office. I'll be there in a moment." I picked up the phone at Peter's desk and called down to the sound stage. Peter answered, his voice barely audible above the noise the men around him were generating. "Peter, I have something to take care of in my office. Keep the boys down there happy until I get back, okay?"

"Yes, Sir, Mr. MacKenna!"

I went into my office, locking the door behind me. This wasn't going to take long, but I didn't want to be interrupted. I thought I'd feel bad about what I was planning to put the kid through, but I didn't. I love sex and, even if the kid wasn't my type, I knew I'd enjoy fucking him. If things turned out the way I expected, it would get him out of my hair for good.

He was in my private bathroom. I could hear water running in the sink. "I'll be right out," he called.

"Make it fast," I said impatiently. "I haven't got all day, kid. What's your name, anyway?"

"Alec." The water stopped running and he came out of the bathroom, drying his hair with one of my monogrammed towels.

I couldn't believe the kid's gall. Using my bathroom without asking me, then helping himself to one of my expensive towels. I had been annoyed with him before, but now I was downright pissed.

"You've got a lot of nerve—!" I started, but my anger quickly faded when I saw Alec's head emerge from under the towel. It was now a mass of soft curls reaching just to his neck. He looked as if he'd just ridden down Pacific Coast Highway with the top down. Windblown—and very sexy.

"Big improvement," I admitted, then pointed to his glasses. "Can you see anything without those?"

"Depends how close you let me get."

I let the remark pass and told him to take them off. When he did, I found myself staring into eyes that were such a clear, deep blue I could have drowned in them. The large, ugly eyeglass frames had been covering a face I could have called handsome, but his soft, gentle features made beautiful a much better word. I stared at him, wondering how I could have been so easily fooled by such a simple disguise. Without the glasses, and with his hair back to its natural curly state, he looked like a totally different person. The removal of the glasses alone had produced such a transformation that I suddenly understood how Clark Kent had been able to fool the citizens of Metropolis.

"Much better," I said honestly. "Now let's see what you look like out of those clothes."

Alec began to undress. His movements were slow, deliberate, and blatantly sexual. I felt as if I were watching a professional stripper at work. The tie went first, then the jacket, and finally his shirt, until he was naked from the waist up.

He was slight in build, and lean. His pecs were well-defined, but not overly developed, and the absence of any chest hair gave his man's body a hint of boyishness I liked. His nipples, a deep burgundy against his pale skin, jutted out from his chest, each small nub of flesh pierced and decorated by a gold nipple ring.

I've always made my videos to fuel men's imaginations as well as their desires, and when I saw those gold nipple rings against Alec's pale skin, I began to envision a tale about a young American who'd been transported to the Arabian desert in a distant century. Abandoned in a foreign land, he had been rescued by a wealthy and mysterious sheik and become the man's favorite concubine. The moment I cast Alec in that role, I knew the audition had already ended.

But I found I still wanted him, so I said only: "Very nice. Now let's see the rest of you."

Alec smiled coyly, and continued with the unveiling, obviously intending to save the best for last. He unlaced and kicked off his shoes, then peeled off his socks. His hands lingered at his belt a moment before he opened it and pulled it through his belt loops. Finally he unzipped his fly, and with a flourish, lowered his pants and stepped out of them.

I hadn't been so surprised by the contents of a package since my fifth birthday when I'd watched with delight as a model train had emerged from its wrapping paper. But I knew I was going to enjoy playing with this boytoy more than I ever had with that train.

Rather than the boxer shorts I had expected, Alec was wearing a black silk thong. He was standing sideways, allowing me to see the rich curve of his buttocks. Then he turned his back to me so I could get the full effect. That's when I saw the tattoo. It was on his right asscheek, a dark red rose, with a single drop of blood falling from a thorn on its stem. That tat looked so hot against his pale cheek that I began to picture it on screen. It would look beautiful by the light of a campfire, the flickering flames illuminating the harem boy's ass as he performed a seductive dance for his sheik's pleasure. Just watching the scene unfold in my mind had my mouth dry and my cock stirring.

When Alec knew I'd had enough time to get a good look at the tattoo, he turned around so I could get a better look at his full, silk-covered basket. "Take that thing off," I ordered. Alec obeyed immediately, pulling down the thong and stepping out of it.

There was nothing boyish about his cock. It was more than ample for a guy his size. I was pleased to see he was semi-erect, his strip-tease having excited him as much as it had me. His cockhead, the same rich color as his nipples, leaked a pearl of precum from the slit. His small ballsac was as hairless as his chest, and already lifted up slightly in his excitement.

Any plans I'd had for a quick fuck vanished. Now that I had seen Alec naked, I wanted more, much more.

I got up from my chair and reached behind him, running my hands down his smooth back. I cupped his asscheeks in my large hands and boosted him up, forcing Alec onto his toes. He put his hands on my shoulders to steady himself, then used his hold to raise himself up to my greater height. I kissed him, a long, lingering, wet kiss. My tongue poked at his teeth, requesting entrance, and when he opened his mouth, our tongues battled for position. I won, and thrust my tongue down his throat.

I let Alec down and started to unbutton my shirt, but he pushed my hands away and ripped it open. He pulled his lips from mine, and put his mouth on my chest, moving over the area the shirt had been covering. Alec trailed his tongue through the thick forest of hair that covered my chest till he had found my nipples. He took possession of them, sucking them, biting them, uncovering them only long enough to bath them in his hot breath. My cock pushed against my zipper.

My own breath escaped my chest in short gasps.

He released my nipples, and his mouth moved down my stomach, leaving a trail of saliva on my burning skin. All the while his fingers worked feverishly to undress me fully. He got my slacks unbuttoned and opened my fly; then, hooking his fingers into the waistband of my shorts, pulled both underwear and pants down in one swift motion. My cock sprang free, fully engorged. I stepped out of the clothing at my feet and kicked it aside.

Alec sank to his knees and stared and, after a moment, reached out to touch me, his finger tracing every inch of my tool. He cradled my heavy ballsac in his hand, then placed his cheek against my hot flank and let his tongue follow the same path his finger had just traveled. He pulled himself away only long enough to reach inside his brief-case and pull out a condom. Watching Alec rip open the wrapper made my body tremble in anticipation. He kissed my cockhead with reverence, then rolled the latex down over my hard shaft and took me in his mouth.

His mouth took possession of my cock the same way it had my upper body. His lips and tongue beguiled me, lulling me into a passive role. Swallowing me halfway, he moved up and down my shaft, licking the underside in slow, agonizing strokes. It made me feel so weak in the knees that I had to rest my ass against my desk for support. When Alec released me I groaned and reached out to pull him back onto my cock.

He escaped my attempt to grab him, but returned on his own, his tongue darting out like a viper, attacking first my cockhead, then the sensitive skin under my balls. I endured the exquisite torture for as long as I could, then I took my revenge, taking his head between my hands and prodding my erection against his lips. When he opened his mouth, I thrust my cock inside. I fucked his mouth savagely, burying my fingers in his curls as I buried my cock in his throat. Few men have been able to handle my girth, but Alec took me down to the base without gagging.

Giving his mouth such a hard workout was pushing me to the edge quickly. I felt the familiar stirring in my balls, the pulsing in my legs that always preceded my orgasms. Alec seemed to know I was ready before I did. He pulled back, dislodging me from his throat, and I groaned in frustration. "Not yet," Alec said, quickly placing his thumb and forefinger right below my cockhead and squeezing once, twice, three times. My urgency quickly dissipated.

Alec stood up and turned around. Brushing aside the papers in the middle of my desk, he lay face down over it, lifting his arms up over his head and opening his legs wide in complete surrender. I moved behind him, once again delighting in the sight of his beautiful young ass. I reached up and held both of his wrists in one hand while I kissed the back of his neck. With my other hand I stroked his asscheeks, spreading them, fluttering my finger down his crack. Alec shivered. He was mine for the taking, but I didn't want him, at least not this way. I took hold of Alec's shoulders and gently turned him over. "I want you on your back," I told him. "I want to see your face when I make you come."

I leaned down and kissed him, slipping my hand under his ballsac to find the puckered skin at the entrance to his asshole. I pushed one finger in tentatively. Alec's mouth came away from mine with a gasp. His opening was small and tight, and as hot at the midday sun. I pushed his knees tight against his chest and hooked his legs over my shoulders, giving me a full view of his tiny, pink hole. Placing my cock at the entrance, I pushed against it until I was able to get the head inside. Then I began a slow advance.

Alec's was no virgin hole, but it was still difficult for him to handle a cock as large as mine. He was whimpering and shifting uncomfortably under me immediately. I put my hands on his hips to steady him and went on. As I made my way inside him, Alec moved his head from side to side, his eyes closed, his lips moving silently. Sweat gleamed on his taut belly as he strained to stay with me. It took all my will power just to keep from giving in to my desire to ram my cock up Alec's ass, my need to possess him was so strong.

Just when I was sure he wouldn't be able to take any more of me, he gave a small cry and his muscles yielded. My cock slid into him, further and further until his asshole had swallowed me whole. He stared up at me, his eyes wide with desire. "Fuck me," he said weakly.

I began with small thrusts, letting him get accustomed to the fullness in his ass, then I began to move in and out of him. My cock seemed to grow with each thrust, sending me deeper and deeper into him until I felt as if his body was an extension of my own. I leaned down to cover his left nipple with my mouth. Taking the ring carefully between my teeth, I tugged gently. Alec let out a moan of pure lust. Seeing the unbridled rapture in his face brought as much pleasure to my eyes as his ass was bringing to my cock.

I began to thrust harder and faster, my large low-hangers slapping loudly against Alec's ass with each stroke. The initial shock of my entry had caused Alec to go soft, but now he was rockhard again, his erection standing straight up between us. I wrapped my left hand around his cock and began to jerk him off.

He was moving with me now, lifting his hips up to meet me, his ass muscles clamping down on my cock with each thrust. When I knew I couldn't hold back any longer, I reached down with my right hand and gave his ass a quick slap. He cried out again, and his cock leapt around wildly in my hand, spewing out strands of milky liquid. I erupted inside Alec a second later, my entire being centered in my cock as wave after wave of cum flowed from my balls into the rubber. My release seemed endless, draining all my stamina, until finally, when I had no more to give, I collapsed on top of him, my heart racing wildly, my breath coming in short pants.

Eventually, I gathered enough strength to move and lifted myself off him, gently lowering his legs from my shoulders. Then I fell back into the soft leather seat of my desk chair and peeled off the condom, dropping it into the wastebasket under my desk.

He seemed as exhausted as I was. He lay still, his face flushed, his cock limp between his legs. I could see his pulse beating in his spent balls. "So, Mr. MacKenna," he asked, "did I pass the audition?"

"Kiddo," I told him wearily, "you not only passed, you got an A+." With great effort, I got out of my chair, offered Alec my hand, and helped him up.

"So I'll get my screen test?" he asked.

"Yes, you'll get it—" I let the rest of my words trail off as I remembered. "Actually," I told him, "you already did."

"What do you mean?" he asked.

I crossed the room, surprised to find my cock was already beginning to revive. It swung out in front of me as I moved, Alec's eyes following it greedily. Going to the large bookcase, I took three books down from the middle shelf. The video camera they had been hiding was now visible.

He stared at me, unbelieving. "You taped us fucking?"

"Not intentionally," I explained. "It's a security camera. I turned it on when I thought I'd be out of the office for the rest of the day. I could have turned it off when we came in, but I didn't expect we'd be very long."

"You never really intended to give me a chance, did you?" he asked.

"No," I said honestly, "but then something happened, something I never expected. You moved me, kid, in a way no one has in a very long time." I took the cassette out of the camera and replaced the books on the shelf. "You're going to get your shot, Alec, but not with this tape. I'm saving this for my personal viewing only."

As I came back to my desk, Alec said softly, "Then you'll have something to remember me by—" He hesitated, his eyes searching mine. "Unless you'd like a repeat performance."

"I think I need one," I said, trying to sound as serious as I could, "just to make sure you can maintain the same level of concentration you had today." I took a business card from my desk and wrote my home address and phone number on the back, then handed it to him.

When Alec read the card he looked up at me, a sly smile on his lips. "I'm sure I'll be able to, Mr. MacKenna—under your direction."

I laughed out loud and told him, "Congratulations, kid, and welcome to Hard Epic Videos. I'll have the contracts drawn up tomorrow, but for now—"

I pulled Alec into my arms, and we sealed the deal with a kiss.

Cock Rock

Murray Brown

I FELT SOMEONE WATCHING ME AND WAS PRETTY SURE I KNEW WHO IT was.

I shook my sun-streaked hair so that it framed my cheekbones as I swiveled under the spotlight, using my guitar like a shield.

For two years now, people had been coming to JD's Tavern to watch me. They came to hear me sing songs that rang of rage and desire. They came to dance and dream to Separate Refuge and press against the edge of the small stage. Being watched was part of the package.

This was different. Only, I felt no malice—just a cool curiosity.

The bastard was sitting at the end of the stage—just beyond the floodlights. I was right. It was him again.

The dark-haired man had come in every night for a week. He always sat alone. He seemed unaffected by the music. He didn't drink and he didn't flirt with the hunks who were always walking past his table. The man just sat and watched me. I felt the heat of his dark eyes boring through the smoke and the haze right to the center of my hammering heart.

I was hot tonight, like I was anytime I was on stage. I gripped the neck of the Fender Telecaster as if it were a lifeline. The bass penetrated the darkness beyond the stage. The drums built up a buffer separating me from the real world. I clutched my guitar and wailed through my last song for the night.

The lights were on in the bar. I licked my lips and cased the crowd. The man sat alone at the end of the stage and continued to watch me. It was late Saturday night and Separate Refuge needed to be packed up and put away again.

I took a swig of lukewarm soda from the bottle stashed behind the drum kit. "New boyfriend?" the drummer asked. "Don't let Jerry know," he said with a smirk.

Jerry managed Separate Refuge. Jerry had managed me these past two years. I didn't think much about Jerry, though—not since he announced we were over and I was moving out of Jerry's bed and house. But Jerry did keep the checks coming. I kept hoping he'd come back to me, too.

"Jerry doesn't own me." I eased the Fender Telecaster into its case. "And, I don't have a boyfriend, new or otherwise." I blushed and fumbled with my equipment.

He was still watching me. I turned and gazed directly at the man who had tormented me the past week. I saw a slim, attractive man in dark clothes. A line describing Lord Byron—"mad, bad, and dangerous to know"—popped into my head. My blush deepened as I imagined I heard the stranger chuckling at my discomfort.

"So, who is tall, dark, and whatever?" the drummer asked, jerking his head towards the man.

"I don't know him."

"You will," the drummer chuckled and began disassembling his drums. "If nothing else, he's invested a lot of time in staring at you this week."

I shrugged.

"Don't you get it?" the drummer asked as he took a step toward the steps at the back of the stage. "Dude comes in every night this week, always alone—doesn't drink, doesn't dance, doesn't talk—just checks you out."

I went through an elaborate display of unplugging the double stacked amplifiers.

The club was closing, the lights had already been dimmed. Most of the crowd had already drifted out. Picking up my guitar, I turned and finally made eye contact with the dark-haired man standing at the end of the stage. The stranger had broad shoulders and narrow hips. And long legs displayed in form-fitting jeans stretched out beneath the table. The man smiled in a way that said: I know your secret. He was the kind of man I wanted, the kind I'd thought Jerry was until that little bubble burst over me.

I was zapped into fantasyland, imagining what it'd be like to get it on with him. Instantly, I needed the man like there was no tomorrow.

"Are you going to take all night to get your shit together?" the man asked as he leaned on the stage. "I'm waiting for you."

I white-knuckled the guitar case and moved closer. "If I am going crazy," I mumbled to myself, "at least, the voices are friendly."

I found myself being pulled to the end of the stage. Towards the man. Towards whatever he offered. He was obviously enjoying himself. He shoved an empty chair towards me with the toe of his boot and sat back down. "I've been here every night this week. Aren't you the least bit curious?"

I sank into the chair.

"Jon Lewiston," the stranger announced, giving me a firm handshake. He didn't let go of my hand; with his free hand, he flicked a black business card with white script across the table.

I picked it up. "Film?" I asked, seeing the design of the card but unable to make out the words in the dimness that was now JD's Tavern.

"I direct for Global Entertainment. I've been wondering if you'd be interested in branching out? You're hot on stage; if you can deliver in front of a camcorder as well, I could use you."

"A camcorder?" I asked hesitantly, trying to adjust to this new direction that was so different than what I'd been expecting. "What kind of movies do you make?"

Jon chuckled and, caressing my palm idly, said: "The triple X kind—gay porn."

I felt a jolt of electricity run from my hand to my prick. Jon's finger kept rhythmically stroking my palm and he stared at me with world-weary, dark, smokey eyes. I could hardly breathe, I was suddenly afraid Jon would disappear and I would be alone in my room at Aunt Esther's house beating off under the quilt. Or, maybe, I would wake up on my couch with the empty TV screen sputtering after the end of another video where gorgeous studs had at each other.

"Don't you guys run ads or something?" I asked.

"Sometimes." His voice sounded strained, as if he hadn't expected me to question his approach. He drummed his fingers on the table. "Want to give it a try?"

"What would I have to do?" I kept my voice steady.

"Me." Jon smiled and leaned forward as if he was going to kiss me. An inch away from my lips he stopped.

I felt my stomach tighten, I rubbed my thighs together. Porn? Me do porn? It sure wasn't what I was thinking of when I joined this man at his table. I was thinking I wanted him. Him and me. Him making me feel good like Jerry used to do. Like I hadn't felt since. I gazed into Jon's waiting, watching eyes. Why the fuck not? I could get away from Charlotte and be free. I could even have this Jon Lewiston, probably pretty much when I wanted him. I leaned forward and my lips touched his.

Instantly, I was devouring Jon's mouth, my tongue probing and then thrusting with a primal rhythm. Still holding my guitar beside me, I deepened the kiss.

The man's fingers rose from the table to touch my face. They moved to grip the back of my head, holding me to him as our tongues dueled.

I leaned back then, breaking the kiss and forcing myself to smile. "So, do I get the part?"

"We'll see," he gasped as he sat back and studied me. "There's more to it than just a kiss and shaking your tight butt on stage," he said as his gaze fell to my lips. He visibly forced his thoughts back to his stated purpose for being at JD's Tavern, blotting out everything else and immersing himself in the role of talent scout. Even so, I had seen his interest. I had felt it as he kissed me. Interest in me as me, not as just a piece of ass for his cameras.

"If you're free tomorrow afternoon, we could do a test—if you're up for it."

"I'm up for anything." I licked my lips slowly, the tip of my tongue just barely exposed, playing it cool.

"The studio's address is on my card," Jon Lewiston said. "Can you make it at three tomorrow?"

I couldn't see his face well in the bar's dimness; I didn't have a clue what the man was thinking. I wanted to kiss him again. I wanted a lot more than kisses. "I can make it anytime," I answered huskily.

I drove back to Aunt Esther's only half-watching the road. I let myself into my room still cursing myself for leaving the bar alone. I fell across the bed and shoved my head under the pillow. "Shit!" I growled against the mattress. I'd convinced myself it was just the guy's job, scouting out men who wanted to get it on in front of the camera. But, still... I could've gotten a fuck off Jon Lewiston tonight—if I'd played my cards right, instead of trying to be so cool.

Maybe it *was* just doing his job for Jon Lewiston. But, could it be something else? There had seemed to be a different message in the way he wove his fingers through my hair when we kissed and the way his tongue had thrust deep into my mouth, exploring it possessively.

I didn't care about being in a movie—not really. I loved my music. I loved performing. And Jerry was promising better was just around the corner. I just knew I wanted Jon Lewiston. He was the man I'd been waiting for ever since Jerry sent me packing. I couldn't get the man out of my thoughts. If it took fucking on stage, that'd be okay; I'd come pretty close to that, doing shit Jerry suggested when I first started out. I'd do it—cameras and all—to get Jon Lewiston's dick in my ass.

I pulled my hard cock out of my briefs to give it breathing room. Doing so started me imagining undressing Jon, my lips and tongue exploring the man's body lovingly. I stroked myself as my thoughts had me getting up on my knees to help the man get to my hole easily. Even when I'd come all over the sheets and my pole had gone soft, I couldn't get Jon Lewiston out of my mind. I could almost feel him still buried deep in my butt.

It was nearly noon when I awoke and I felt as if I hadn't slept more than a few minutes. I tried to tell myself I shouldn't go to the director's office—not to try out for his porn movie. I tried to ignore my piss-hard-on. And failed at both. I eventually surrendered to the inevitable and, climbing out of bed, moved to the bathroom attached to my bedroom.

Trying on and rejecting four different pairs of jeans, I decided on a tight pair that showed off my bulge and ass, a pair that Jerry had given me when I was just starting and we were still fucking—before Jerry decided he liked women and I had to move in with Aunt Esther.

I found the address on Jon's card—an old warehouse on the river. It was Sunday afternoon and there were only a few cars on the street. Parking in front of the building, I checked my hair in the rearview mirror before studying the warehouse carefully.

The main entrance into the warehouse was unlocked and Global Entertainment was the second suite. I knocked on the door gingerly.

He opened the door immediately, dressed in black jeans and an oxford shirt. He smiled when he saw me. "Good to see you," he said and cupped my elbow, leading me into the anteroom.

"I want a kiss," I told him as soon as the door was closed behind us, and pulled the man to me. My doubts had fled the moment that I had him before me again. My lips pressed against his, my tongue prying his teeth open. I felt his hands circle my waist and sighed as our kiss became deep.

This was right. Jon Lewiston was right. For me. No matter what I had to do to get him. To have him.

Jon pulled away from the kiss, his hands descending to my asscheeks and stopping there to hold them. He smiled. "You are a hungry one, aren't you?"

I blushed. "It's been—a while."

"What does your manager say about you getting into porn movies? he asked as he led me into a large office.

"Jerry doesn't know." I frowned at the thought of the man. "We've never recorded. We don't seem to be going anywhere..."

"You haven't?" There was genuine amazement in his voice. "But, you're so good."

"Jerry says we have to create more of a buzz before he can market us to the labels."

He indicated the couch to me. "I don't see how much more of a buzz you could create. The band is ready to take off. You really have magic on stage. Are you sure this guy knows what he's doing?"

I shrugged and sat down. I looked back up at Jon and hoped he wanted something to happen as much as I did.

"Well?" His word hung in the still air.

"He says he does." I drummed my fingers on my thigh nervously. "He says we have to be ready."

"Do you and this Jerry have a thing going then?"

"We sort of did, I guess—a couple of years ago," I admitted, looking down at my hands. "Not any more, though." I shrugged and licked my lips, imagining what lay under the black jeans in front of me.

Jon nodded and cleared his throat. "You ready to let me see your stuff?" I looked up sharply. "See if you've got what it takes to be a pornstar?"

"Whatever," I mumbled. Yeah—whatever I need to do to get close to you, I thought.

"Okay, let me give you the scenario—you come into a music shop to buy—oh, I don't know—guitar strings. I come up behind you and ask you if you've found what you're looking for. You turn around and look at me—and answer: I have now. We take it where it goes from there. You're going to have to trust me on my feel for how you're playing it—maybe you're star material, maybe you aren't." Jon wiped his palms on his pants. "Use my desk as the layout for the strings, okay?"

"That's it? No script or anything?" I gnawed my lip as I stood up and crossed to the desk.

"That's it. You want it enough to try for it?"

My mouth was dry. "Yeah, I want it," I answered as he moved over to the door, giving me the office in which to develop the scenario in my mind. His sleek black jeans cupped his high, firm ass; the play of muscles in his butt was outlined in heart-stopping detail. His feline movements mesmerized me. At least I'll have one time with him, I told myself. I'll get laid by the guy I want. And I'll finally be free. I won't ever be Jerry's discarded boy again.

I stood before the desk, forcing myself to pretend there was something there I wanted, something as dumb as guitar strings.

Thick carpeting muffled the sound of Jon's boots. His breath ruffled the tiny hairs on the back of my neck as he came up behind me. "Find what you came in for?" he asked.

It took me an eternity to pivot. "I have now," I said, looking into his dark, smoky eyes. Melting into those eyes and the promise of freedom they held.

I ran my fingers through the hair over Jon's ears, moving toward the back of his head and pulling him closer. We came together, pressing against each other's groin. I took possession of his mouth, beginning with a soft lick across his lips and then a slow nibble that built into a deep, open-mouthed tongue duel. My hands slipped over Jon's shoulders and down his back, pushing his shirt off him.

I pulled back and studied the man in my arms. Dark eyes watching mine, hard cock against mine, hands possessing my butt. I placed a series of butterfly kisses down his neck before licking the sweet spot where his collarbone stood out in sharp relief.

I felt Jon's dick struggling against its cloth prison. I unsnapped his jeans, frantic in my haste to grasp it in my hand. I moved my hand back and forth along the length of the shaft, through the cotton of the briefs, as my lips pressed kisses from the man's collarbone to the center of his throat. My fingers made forays along his shaft until they found the head of his rigid pole. My touch alternated between whisper soft and the edge of pain. A hot, sweet rhythm pulsed through my veins as pure as the blues. Dancing to music only I heard, I unbuttoned Jon Lewison's oxford shirt and began to feast on the salty flesh. I suckled his nipples and he moaned. His body began to grind with me.

I was taking what I had wanted for so long, claiming the freedom I needed—what I thought I had found in those first hot, sex-filled weeks with Jerry so long ago. Before the man left me alone and returned to a woman.

Even as the memory touched my mind, I rejected it. I didn't want any clouds on the horizon now that I had Jon. Now that I was going to make love to this man as I had needed to for so long. Now that I would finally be free—of Aunt Esther. Of Jerry. Of everything and everyone who'd kept me in Charlotte.

Grabbing the sides of Jon's jeans and briefs with both hands, I fell to my knees, pulling them down along his legs. I engulfed Jon's aching manhood in my throat. Swirling my tongue around and under the swollen helmet, I began to bob my head slowly back and forth.

Clutching Jon's hips, I pulled him deep into my throat until my nose was buried in his pubes. Moving my head quickly back, I left every inch of the man's pole exposed to the tepid air while I flicked my tongue lightly across the helmet.

I continued my ministrations until the air was heavy with sex and the room could barely contain the need that was freeing me as it consumed me.

Jon grabbed my head and pulled it off his cock. Shaking, he fell to his knees and hugged me to him. "I want to fuck you," he whispered as his tongue found my ear. His fingers worked the button loose at my waist and unzipped my fly. Gingerly, he began to move the tightly stretched fabric down over my backside.

"Let me help you," I mumbled and, standing up, pulled off my shirt as Jon got my jeans and briefs down to my ankles.

Jon reached to his own jeans for a condom as I pulled my clothing over my feet and walked naked to the couch.

I could feel his face stretched in a wide smile. I felt an itch deep in my ass, blazing now that it almost had relief. I sat down on the couch and raised my legs, watching him kneel before me. I lay back against the couch and shut my eyes as my feet were positioned behind his neck. "Take it slow and easy," I told him, "I want to enjoy this one for all it's worth."

I felt the wide latex-covered helmet establish itself firmly against my entrance and tried to remember how to open myself to it. My ass lifted as Jon's hands pressed down on my thighs to spread them and leaned into me to kiss me. I felt the man's lips against mine and opened my mouth for the tongue prying them apart. I was moments away from freedom. Freedom to be myself and become what I wanted to be.

Pressure mounted against my assmuscle. I remembered that Jerry used to grease me up before he shoved his dick in me and didn't stop until I felt his balls plastered against my asscheeks. I moaned around Jon's tongue and he humped his hips forward.

Pain was a sudden tidal wave rising out of my ass and crashing over me. His helmet pushed through my sphincter and stopped. I realized a moment later we weren't kissing, that his face was inches above mine.

"I'm hurting you?" he asked.

"It's gone now."

"I thought that you—you have been fucked, haven't you?" he asked and wiped tears from my eyes with his thumbs. I nodded. "How long has it been?"

"Almost two years now."

I could see the lights go on in his eyes. "You've only made it with one guy, too, I'll bet—and that was your asshole agent, right?" I nodded again. "I don't want to hurt you, Eric. Do you want me to pull out?"

"No!" I growled. "Fuck me. Make the past go away, make me free of it." I looked up into his eyes. "Make me yours, Jon," I whispered.

His fingertip traced from the corner of my eye down along my cheek to my lips. "You're what I want, baby—what I need." He lowered his face to mine, his lips brushing mine as I felt him begin to ease the rest of the way into me.

I gasped as his cockhead massaged my joyspot and grabbed his face to pull his lips hard against mine as his shaft continued the massage inch after inch. My cock sprang to attention and threatened to erupt as his abs caressed its helmet while his hips pulled his shaft back along my prostate. "Fuck me," I moaned around his tongue.

He raised his head and smiled down at me as he found his rhythm. "I'm never going to just fuck you, Eric. But I'm going to make love to you as many times a day as you'll let me." Wordlessly, he watched me and I watched him as his cock moved in and out of my ass in long, slow strokes. I reached up and traced the line of his lips with a finger as he moved in me and my cock began to ooze. He reached between us and wrapped his hand around me, stroking me in time with his rhythm in my gut.

My balls tightened against my shaft as he slowly continued to stroke me. My cock expanded and I was seeing stars as I shot a load that hit his chest. Another volley hit my cheek. My gut flexed and clinched at his dick in time with my explosions. I felt his thighs and groin push hard against my asscheeks and became still as his pole expanded deep inside me. I felt the pulses of his own ropes of jizz spraying into the rubber, filling it up.

He collapsed on top of me and I reached around my legs to hold each of his asscheeks in my hands. Our breathing was ragged and both of us were sapped of our strength. We lay locked together like that and I was finally free.

You've got the part, Eric," he whispered against my ear. I froze and he felt it. "The part as my lover—if you want it." I relaxed. "I promise I won't ever hurt you, baby."

We sat beside each other on the couch, our bodies pressed together. "Tomorrow, we'll get rid of Jerry."

"Who's going to manage me?" I asked.

"Me."

I smiled at Jon Lewiston and knew I was finally free of my past.

Stairway To Stardom

J.D. Ryan

"LOOK, PAL, IF I WANTED AN AUDIENCE, I'D YODEL!" I COULD FEEL MY temper slipping. Damned kids, always so certain they were the next star Armand Bettencourt needed. I was tired of them mobbing my studio, and I damn well wouldn't put up with one interrupting my vacation.

He'd trailed me long enough. If this kept up, I'd have to start using an alias for hotel stays. I glared back at my young follower. He smirked at me from his perch on the back of the wrought iron park bench. He'd wrapped his arms around his parted knees, offering me a glimpse of the barely covered basket between.

Why did hustlers always think a man wanted skin-tight shorts that showed everything? I would have more class, if I wanted to sell myself. I turned my attention back to the crumpled tour brochure in my fist. This was my first time in South Carolina, and I was going to enjoy everything that Charleston had to offer. Besides, when you're a good director, any new experience might stimulate your creativity.

The tourist brochure suggested that I visit a historic house during the hot part of the day. That suited my plans—I doubted my young tag-along would follow past the ticket booth. The nearest such house on the map, the Aiken-Rhett House, should be a mere three blocks to my right. I turned resolutely in that direction, ignoring the sticky film of sweat that had covered me since my arrival. After all, as the locals kept reminding me: it wasn't the heat, it was the humidity.

Ten minutes of struggling through Charleston's humidity brought me to my destination. I stood at the gate for a long moment, one eyebrow cocked. The Aiken-Rhett House seemed badly in need of funding. Its peeling plaster had once, I thought, been the color of ripe peaches. Patches of it had fallen away in spots, revealing crumbling bricks beneath and making the house look like it was molting.

I slung the camera bag around to my back and climbed the oddly proportioned marble staircase. People must have had smaller feet in those days. White marble, too—must have been a bitch to keep clean.

I glanced behind me as I banged the brass knocker against its polished plate. The kid smiled hopefully from beneath a palmetto tree, both thumbs hooked in the waistband of those skin-tight shorts. He flipped his long, black hair over one shoulder with a move I had to admit was graceful. I scowled, a curse rising in my throat.

I swallowed the curse as I heard the massive door creak. It was hauled open by a tiny old lady who looked like she might've been as old as the house. I didn't see how she managed to budge the thick oak. I slipped inside, where a blast of air conditioning hit me like a wall of ice. I could almost feel the sweat freezing.

The woman led me up yet another small set of white marble steps, explaining that the original citizens had built upwards to catch the sea breezes. In a proper Charlestonian mansion, the first floor was actually the second. She led me past an impressive, curving staircase and deposited me in an ornate parlor—after relieving me of the tour fee, of course—to await the next scheduled tour.

I glanced out the window. My tag-along was nowhere in sight. With a satisfied smirk, I circled the room, reading the placards mounted at strategic locations. I was lucky, I read, to be able to tour an authentic mansion in the process of being "restored." I shrugged, peering out the door for another look at the great curving stairs. Before and after photos would have been fine with me. The room across the hall was less lavishly decorated than the parlor. I could see peeling wallpaper and a faded rug. I checked my watch; still over half an hour until the next tour.

I am not a patient man. But if I left the building now, I might find my young stalker hiding behind the nearest oleander bush. I stepped into the hall, ready to duck back inside if the old lady spotted me.

A battered, oddly slender door hid in the shadows behind the grand staircase. I stuck my head inside. There, hidden in the walls of the building, was the oddest set of stairs I'd ever seen. So steep they were very nearly a ladder, and so narrow that my shoulders brushed the wall on either side. I had no idea what they were for—thus, I had to find out where they led.

Once I pulled the door shut behind me, I truly appreciated electricity. Only a small window set a little above my head lighted the stairway. The door fastened with a simple hook and eye, which I flipped shut. No sense having my snooping interrupted.

I fought my way up the stairs, arriving in a sitting room on the third floor (which was the second, if viewed from the local perspective). I pulled out the camera for a few shots of the ornate Victorian sofa, envisioning finely dressed gentlemen making love in front of the fireplace. Huge windows faced a balcony that ran the length of the house. I stepped closer to find that the panes slid into the ceiling, making a doorway onto the balcony. I could, indeed, feel a cool breeze from the ocean—and catch a glimpse of the next room, where I could see a small knot of tourists heading for the stairs. I ducked back into the sitting room.

The teenager stood just inside the doorway, one slender hand resting on the back of the sofa. For a moment, even my brilliant wit eluded me. I stood with my mouth open, unable to believe my eyes. Then, my blood began to boil.

"How did you—?" I sputtered.

He grinned, perfect white teeth sparkling against bronze skin. "I told the old biddy I had an urgent message for the famous director."

"What part of the word 'no' don't you understand?" I snapped.

He cringed back a step when I stomped toward the narrow doorway. At least he had the brains to worry. I scowled, then brushed roughly past him.

"So I'm not worth a second glance, is that it?" he called softly after me.

I paused, struck by something in the smooth voice. All right, maybe I remembered another young hustler trying to make it in the glitz and glamour of the LA film business. I turned to study the youngster. He had the most startling green eyes, hooded by lashes thick enough to make a woman jealous. But they held old pain like faded photographs. This one was a true street rat, not the smooth boy-salesmen I was used to. This one's sort sold his body to stay alive.

That might be an interesting change from the sophisticated models I'd been using—what was I thinking? I shook my head, turning for the door.

"Tell you what, kid: you show up at the studio, prove you're legal, and we might work something out."

"I'm legal," he muttered.

I rolled my eyes. "When was the last time you saw chicken in a Bettencourt film?"

Silence. I glanced back. He'd dug his driver's license from somewhere in those painted-on shorts, and his fingers still held it out in my direction. His shoulders had sagged, though. The plastic card started to slip. I sighed and snatched it before it fell to the floor.

I stared out the window, watching the leaves of the palm tree sway in the sea breeze. What was I getting myself into? I didn't need to start adopting strays, for crying out loud! My gaze dropped to the card in my hand. J.T. Pierce... turned 18 three months ago. I closed my eyes.

"All right," I heard my voice growl, "you've got one chance to impress me." I tried to glower at the teenager. I crossed my arms and gave him my best crabby director look while hope bloomed in his eyes.

"Where do you want to go?"

I held up one finger. "I didn't say we were going anywhere, pal. You've got one chance... here... now."

His Adam's apple bobbed. His eyes widened, then narrowed. "And if I impress you—?"

I chuckled. "That's one big 'if,' but..." I looked him over, this time with a professional eye. Thin, but wiry rather than scrawny; he'd have the strength to last through a day's shooting. That bronze skin hinted at Latino or Native American ancestors, but those green eyes... An exotic mix, interesting enough to work with. Now to see if he knew how to use the body properly.

"If you impress me," I finished, "we'll go back to LA, and I'll put you in my next picture." I paused, waiting until his grin faded. "And I'll take the plane fare out of your first paycheck."

His gaze darted around the room, lighting on the sofa. I leaned against the wall. He was going to pick some run-of-the-mill fuck scene and I'd be off the hook. I watched him run a hand over the velvet upholstery. He turned, glanced back at me. I gave him no clue— no grin, no frown, no shrug.

He shook his head. "Not a casting couch," he murmured. "Too easy."

My eyebrow rose. Maybe the kid did have some talent. His gaze settled somewhere just over my right shoulder. I turned. The narrow doorway.

"The old slave stairs," J.T. said softly, pulling the door open.

"Is that what it is?" I asked, following him inside. I imagined dark bodies clambering up and down this ladder-like staircase, moving silently behind the walls while their masters lived in opulence less than two feet away from them. I suddenly realized that J.T.'s green eyes were watching my face, reading me like a script.

"I think maybe you'd like that," he whispered. My shoulders tightened—he couldn't have gotten that fact out of any magazine! I'd never acted on any of those fantasies, that's for sure.

He reached behind me to fasten the door, then moved down until he stood in the golden shaft of light from the tiny window. As he glanced back over one shoulder, those green eyes sparkling in the sunlight, I knew I'd need exactly that color of spot for his scenes. His skin almost glowed. "I want to see you naked," I said.

Without a word, he wriggled out of the ridiculous outfit. Then he posed, feet slightly spread, hands behind his back, eyes on the floor. I felt a tingle deep within my balls. In the afternoon sun, he seemed a bronze godling. My mind began to work, even as I stepped closer. I saw a jungle savage seduced by a white trader. I saw an Indian prince on silken pillows. I knew I had to have him.

I ran my hand over the smooth chest, feeling his hard nubs crinkle beneath my palm. His cock was perfectly proportioned, already rising for me, and with such a pretty ballsac that I had to cup my fingers around it. The wiry hairs prickled my hand, and his cock bounced as I squeezed gently. He was uncut, which pleased me. Cut cocks aren't as pretty to me, nor as interesting on film. I watched the pink head slide out of the dark folds of skin, like a flower blooming.

I squeezed his tight, round ass. The muscles clenched under my fingers as he spread his legs wider. I took the invitation. His asshole took two fingers, easily, while he groaned with pleasure. His cock trembled against my trousers.

"All right," I whispered. "Impress me."

"Yes, sir." He grabbed his shorts and slithered past me on the stairs. Fishing a condom packet from a pocket, he ripped it open. He knelt above me, leaning toward the growing tent in my trousers. He hovered there, not moving. I slowly realized he was waiting for a command, and my cock throbbed.

"You may—um—proceed," I muttered. J.T. bent to fasten his lips to my belt buckle. I felt my eyebrow creeping upward as he maneuvered my trousers open without using his hands. Graceful and dexterous—I could work with this combination all right.

Once my cock bobbed free of my clothing, J.T. rolled the condom onto it, again using his mouth rather than his slender fingers. He glanced upwards once, as if to make certain I was watching, then swallowed my shaft in one long gulp. He pressed his face against me, trembling slightly from the effort. I could feel his throat muscles tightening around my cock like a silk glove. I put one hand against the wall, dropping the other into that soft, black mane.

He pulled back slowly, sucking hard. His tongue lapped and teased my shaft, swirled over the head. My fingers clenched in his hair. J.T. impaled himself again, sliding forward to rub his face against my trousers. His tongue darted out, to tease my ballsac. I grunted and gave up trying to control my hips.

He made no move to pull away when I started thrusting into his mouth, merely opened wider to take me. I watched my shaft slide in and out of that pretty mouth, coated with his saliva. J.T. kept his eyes closed, the thick lashes looking like bruises in the dim light.

It took every ounce of self control that I had, but I pulled away before coming. He whimpered, leaning forward, his mouth open.

"Let me see how you take it up the ass," I commanded.

He slipped past me on the stairs, teasing my cock with his asscheeks. He flipped to his back without a sound, as gracefully as I'd come to expect. Bracing his feet against the narrow walls, he presented me with a perfect view of his crinkled hole, ready for my cock. I backed up, moving downstairs until my hips were aligned with his ass. He leaned his head back, groaning as I entered him.

I worked my arms beneath his knees, resting my hands on the steps underneath his shoulders. He grunted as I spread his legs wider, shoving deep within his ass. I watched his face, imagining the camera angle needed to catch his expression as his asshole stretched wide for me. He bit his lip, shook his head from side to side, then threw out his arms to steady himself against my onslaught. When my pubes brushed against his smooth ass, I paused.

J.T. opened those green eyes wide, looking at me like he couldn't believe it. Then he dropped his head back, straightening his arms.

I could feel his wiry muscles tremble beneath me, but it was too late for me to hold in my desire. My hips shoved forward of their own accord, slamming my cock deep within him. My balls slapped against his ass with the pounding rhythm.

He whimpered. His asshole tightened and relaxed, milking my cock. I hauled his legs further up and pinned him against the step. His hands clawed at the walls as my rhythm shoved him upwards, his fingers slipping on the unfinished wood. The sound of his struggle made my balls throb with heat.

I leaned forward until my mouth brushed his silken mane.

"Come," I commanded. I slid one hand between our sweaty bellies until I found his slender cock, slimy with precum.

"Sir," he gasped, writhing beneath me. "Oh, yes!"

I felt him quiver underneath me. I thrust harder, my cock a jackhammer in him. Hot cream spurted over my hand and over our bellies. I milked him, my hand wringing a second, then a third wad from his cock. I kept my fist closed over the shaft, even after it sagged. I could feel my own juices boiling up from my balls.

J.T. gasped when he felt the heat within his canal. I shoved against him, grinding against his butt, as my balls wrung themselves dry. His ass clutched at my shaft, pulling cream from me. When the last quiver ended, I collapsed against the step, too weak to withdraw. He lay limply beneath me, breathing in short pants that ended with a trembling gasp.

I gently lowered his legs from my shoulders. He groaned. I bent forward, my lips finding his soft face. He tasted like the salty, damp breeze that blew through the city. I kissed his eyelids, then moved downward to his mouth. His tongue met mine, each of us still hungry for the other. We ended it only when neither of us could ignore the sticky film that glued us together. I helped him to his feet, and he struggled back into his shorts.

"I'm going to work your ass off," I promised him. "You'll give me every ounce of emotion you possess."

"For the cameras," he added, giving me a quick glance from those startling eyes.

I stared back, wondering—wondering if I dared even ask. But I had to know. "And when the cameras are off?"

J.T. looked at me, his face still. I could see memory surface in his eyes. We studied one another. Hell, I was older—it was up to me to set an example for this damn street rat!

"I want to be with you," I told him, watching the emotions play across his face. When they finally melted into confusion, I spoke again. "I don't know if we can make it work, but I'd like to try."

He tried a small grin. I held out my hand and he looked at it like there might be a knife between my fingers. I held my breath. J.T. swallowed hard, then he slid his hand into mine.

"I might get into that role," he whispered. I pulled him close, drinking in the sweaty, sexy odor of his body.

"You'll be the star," I told him.

Stunt Cock

Bill Crimmin

MATT LOVES TAKING COCK. SHOW HIM SIX INCHES OF GRISTLE AND A
nice set of abs and he practically starts salivating. This is fine by
me—most of the time I'm the guy providing Matt with as much of
his favorite tidbit as he can take. But, if there's one thing I enjoy
almost as much as satisfying his appetite for cock, it's watching him
with another stud.

Don't get me wrong; Matt and I love each other—till death us do
part and all that jazz. And its not like he drops his Calvins for just
anybody—it's business. But it's definitely a case of mixing business
with pleasure. You see, Matt's an exhibitionist and I've always been a
voyeur at heart—so making porn flicks for a living is right up our
alley.

If you've ever watched a gay vid, chances are you've seen us.
Matt's the tall, toned, gorgeous dark-haired guy who comes to re-
place the tap washer, but ends up giving the hero's plumbing a
thorough inspection. Or the cute pizza boy who arrives with a king
size pepperoni and ends up making an extra delivery. I'm sure you
get the picture—photographed in glorious Technicolor and the best
possible taste.

You'll have seen me too—I'm in most of them. What's more I've
always got the biggest part. The most important part, some might say.
But you wouldn't recognize my face. You see, I'm what's known as a
stunt cock.

When you sit on the edge of your seat while Bruce Willis hangs
underneath a helicopter, you know it's really a stuntman taking the
risk. Stuntmen are professionals and, like as not, they'll get the shot
right first time. If Tom Cruise breaks a limb the whole movie has to

be suspended until he recovers but, if the stuntman gets hurt, you just get another one. It's the same in skin flicks.

Long hours acting hard and horny for the cameras can take it out of a guy. It isn't easy achieving an erection to order, or maintaining it until the director is satisfied with the shot. Sometimes, even the most virile member can flag. That's where I step in. Watching handsome, naked guys rolling around on a bed for hours, especially when one of those guys is Matt, especially since I'm a voyeur, brings out the stud in me. By the time I'm called upon to perform the finale I can't wait to come—it's a dirty job but somebody's got to do it.

As you might have guessed, I love my job. Working in porn films provides me with the perfect opportunity to indulge in my favorite form of exercise and get paid for it in the bargain.

Yet it almost didn't happen. If Matt hadn't had a hangover or if I'd decided to stay at home, we'd still be living in a single damp room with the neighbors complaining about the noise every time we played the stereo.

I sat quietly at the back of the studio, listening to the ticking of the wall clock. All the windows were open, but it was stifling. I pulled my damp T-shirt away from my chest and wiped the sweat off my face. I envied Matt, reclining nude on a bed at the front of the room, an electric fan trained directly at him. A semi-circle of easels were arranged round him and about a dozen students worked on their sketches. Just in front of me, a man worked furiously, never taking his eyes off of Matt. His skillful fingers were a blur as a perfect, detailed drawing of my lover began to form on his canvas. He'd caught the curve of the shoulders perfectly and had been careful to draw in the lines that defined the muscles on Matt's belly. And the froth of brown hair that capped the cock, nestling between his taut thighs was lovingly recreated.

The man turned round and looked straight at me. When he saw me staring at his painting, he blushed scarlet. I could see he was captivated by Matt, he could hardly keep his eyes off him.

"It's very good," I said, indicating the painting. "You are talented."

"Thanks," he replied modestly, blushing even redder. "But I can't quite seem to get his chest right. Do you know him?" he asked.

"He's my boyfriend." I replied proudly. I'm used to guys staring at him in the street and women in bars slipping him their phone numbers as they pass by on the way to the ladies'. I've always got rather a kick out of being able to say that he's my boyfriend. I love watching the naked envy in other people's eyes. And this time was no different.

"Would you—? Could you—? I mean would he—?" He started his sentence three or four times, each time fading away into incoherent, embarrassed mumbling. Finally, he took a deep breath, composed himself and asked: "Do you think he'd appear in a movie? It's my day job," he went on. "Painting is just a hobby. I'm an art director in the movie business—porn movies." He added the last two worlds quietly, almost apologetically.

He had my interest now. Matt and I had always enjoyed skin flicks. We had a huge collection at home and regularly used them as part of our foreplay. In fact we had a little fantasy about Matt starring in a porn movie and me being the director. He was an exhibitionist, after all—that was why he worked as a life-model. With me being a closet voyeur, ours was a match made in heaven. After a couple of hours with his clothes off in front of a room full of art students, Matt was always ready for a hot, sweaty session between the sheets. If I tagged along and watched him, so was I.

I knew the prospect of performing in front of the cameras would have Matt practically creaming in his pants. Just thinking about it was making me think about doing the same. What's more, we needed the money. Our lease was up and neither of us was making enough to rent the kind of place we wanted.

"We're interested," I answered confidently. "What do you want us to do?" He gave me his card, wrote the address of a studio on the back and told me he'd like to see Matt at 10:00 am the next day for an audition.

We celebrated a bit too heavily that night on the strength of Matt's new career. Too many beers were drunk, and beer always made me horny. Our extended rehearsal of Matt's audition continued to 4:00 am. Needless to say we rather regretted our binge the next morning. Matt was tired and hungover and his nerve had deserted him. He flatly refused to go to the audition unless I went to hold his hand.

Matt wasn't shy about taking his clothes off, so it wasn't a problem getting naked for the director. I sat quietly at the edge of the set as my lover undressed, trying to see him objectively, to evaluate his appearance as coolly and unemotionally as the director would. He was tall and muscular. His thighs were tapering columns of hard flesh. His shoulders were broad and his chest smooth and defined. Thick black hair tumbled over his brow and gave him a boyish look. He gave the director the treatment—looking directly at him and delivering his killer smile. I'd never been able to resist that smile. My cock hardened in my jeans.

I heard the director take a breath, a long slow breath in through his teeth, and I smiled, knowing he was as hooked as I was.

"Let's see you in action," he said, indicating the bed that was the only furniture on the small set. He beckoned to a young man who had been sitting quietly beside the cameraman. The man stood up, took off a toweling robe, and sat down on the bed.

I could see Matt fancied him; he was just his type. The boy could have been my younger brother. He was about six feet, blond, his broad chest dense with curly hair. Just the way Matt liked them. I could see my lad's eyes light up with anticipation. This is going to be easy, I thought to myself.

The director suggested a simple blow job and I held my breath as Matt settled back on the bed and the other man—James, I learned he was called—positioned himself between Matt's legs.

Matt's cock was already hard by the time the cameras started rolling. James studied it appreciatively. "Just lie back and let me do all the work," he said.

Matt didn't need telling twice. Propping himself up on his elbows he looked down at the blond boy. James leaned forward and tongued the rim of Matt's belly button. He stroked Matt's thighs, trailing his nails over the hard flesh. Matt shivered and his cock gave an involuntary jerk. Things were getting distinctly uncomfortable inside my jeans. I uncrossed my legs, attempting to give my thickening prick more room.

James was giving the sensitive inside of Matt's thighs the fingernail treatment now, all the while licking out his navel. Matt made the little hissing noise that signaled his arousal, and my cock instantly swelled to full erection. Embarrassed, I clamped my hand to my crotch and looked around the room. But all eyes were trained on the bed and nobody noticed the bulge in my jeans. I tried to rearrange it through the denim, but nothing I did seemed to ease my discomfort.

James licked Matt's bollocks, gently sucking and nibbling on his scrotum. My lover's cock stood proudly to attention. The blond man grasped Matt's rod. He pulled back the foreskin, exposing the rosy helmet. A bead of precome glistened on the slit. His tongue licked it away. Matt made the hissing sound again and my engorged dick made its presence felt once more.

It was becoming positively painful. Unconsciously, I began stroking it through the denim. James started licking Matt's shaft. He teased the sensitive underside of Matt's helmet, worked his tongue inside the foreskin and then pulled it back, exposing the glans. He gave Matt's bell-end a thorough tonguing and then slid the tip in his mouth. I'd sucked Matt's cock enough times to know exactly how it must have felt—I could imagine the heat and the silkiness of his skin against my lips.

My jeans were strangling my erection. If I didn't get the circulation going again I'd be risking gangrene. Looking around the room to make sure nobody was looking, I gently eased down my zip and freed my cock. It sprang out, like a jack-in-a-box, the moment I moved my boxers aside. I sighed in relief and grasped it firmly in my hand. I didn't mean to play with it—just to give it some relief from its denim prison. I guess my instincts got the best of me. Pretty soon I found myself slowly wanking as I watched my lover get a thorough blow job from the cute blond boy on the bed with him.

James' face was bobbing up and down on Matt's knob. Taking his meat all the way down to his tonsils and then withdrawing until only the tip was inside his mouth. He was clearly enjoying the experience—his own cock bobbed between his legs as he gobbled Matt. Sliding a hand under Matt's buttocks he wriggled a finger between his cheeks. I saw Matt shiver as one of James' fingers pushed into his hole. I knew how much he loved that, how he'd squirm against my invading finger, forcing it further inside and insisting that I give him a second and a third.

I felt a bit stupid, wanking in an empty warehouse while my boyfriend got sucked off by a total stranger in front of a roomful of people. But a stiff prick has no conscience they say, and I was far too turned on to stop now. Matt was humping James' face as the blond's finger fucked his arsehole.

Seeing Matt fuck someone else, looking at his body from a distance and watching him respond made me appreciate him in a new way. There was something animal about his responses. There was an urgent, overwhelming need about him which was palpable. That, coupled with his good looks, was a winning combination. His face glared out from the video monitor screens like Donatello's David. I gripped my dick in my fist and wanked on.

In fact I was so involved in my own thoughts that I didn't notice that Matt and James had run into problems. James was still mouthing Matt's cock, but I slowly realized that my lover was squirming more with embarrassment than pleasure. And it wasn't arousal that was flushing his cute face a violent crimson, it was shame.

He looked at the director and mumbled apologetically, discomfort making his tongue thick. "I didn't get much sleep last night, and I've got a hangover," Matt told him and it sounded as if he was going to cry. "I'm so sorry—" James sat up and released Matt's cock. To my surprise my usually unashamed lover covered his disloyal genitals with his hand.

I registered all this in seconds. My hand still stroked my cock, without me even thinking about it. Suddenly a voice rang out: "Give me that guy!" I gradually became aware that all the eyes in the room were now trained on me and that the director was pointing directly at me. My hand continued to jerk my John Thomas on autopilot as I looked at them looking at me.

"That's what I need, come here," ordered the director in a voice so authoritative that I dared not disobey. I stood up and stumbled over to the set and sat on the edge of the bed and stroked myself hesitantly as the director barked directions at me: "Slower. Stop a minute. Grip your balls and run your finger over the helmet—"

Finally, after following a series of instructions which had my cock doing everything but dancing the can-can, he told me I could come. I lay back on the bed and let rip. James barely had time to climb between my legs. My crotch was lit up and the cameras began to roll.

A knot of heat gathered in my bollocks and spread through my belly. My dick was pulsating in my hand, on the edge of eruption. My heart fluttered in my chest, sweat poured down my neck, and a deep guttural growl rumbled in my throat. My nuts contracted, pumping out cum as the most violent orgasm I could ever recall shot through my body. Hot spunk spurted across the room and splattered on the wooden floor as wave after wave of pleasure crashed over me.

"Can you do that on demand?" the director asked from beside the bed.

"Yeah," I answered and hoped it was so.

"Good. I need a stunt cock. You'll have to start shaving, of course—but be here tomorrow morning." He turned to face Matt. "Let's see how you look fucking, guy. On the bed."

Matt was on his knees quickly, arse in the air. James was behind him—his eight inches of latex covered man-meat embedding itself in my stud's butt. He gripped Matt's hips and pumped—his dick slid all the way into the tight hole I knew so well. I sat on the edge of the set, my pole rigid again and gripped in my fist as I watched the man I loved get a good dicking.

Seeing him take a cock, watching for the familiar signals and responses, turned me on almost as fucking him myself. I'd just never had the chance to admire his body like this when we were actually on the job. Gazing at his round cheeks, spread apart by a fat cock, and admiring the tautness of his thighs, or the curve of his bicep as he supported his weight, made me appreciate him even more. It sounded stupid, but watching him get porked by another guy seemed to make me love him more intensely (well, I did tell you I was a voyeur, didn't I?).

The camera moved in for a close-up. On the video monitors James's cock seemed huge. Every vein and hair was visible. Drops of moisture clung to the short hairs around Matt's opening and glistened in the bright lights. James continued to ream Matt's arse slowly, the slick pole making slurping noises as it slid in and out. His clenched buttocks moved across the screen as he leisurely fucked my boyfriend's arse. He panted loudly, his hoarse breathing the only sound in the echoing warehouse. A drop of sweat ran down his nose and dropped off onto Matt's back.

I could see the blond was struggling, that he wanted to shoot. The tension in his legs betrayed the effort he was putting into holding back. He followed the director's instructions and ploughed Matt's arse slowly and deliberately, even as he fought the urge to go for the big one.

Finally, satisfied that he had enough footage, the director gave permission for James to pick up speed.

I'm sure I don't need to tell you that in blue movies you always get to see the cum shot. In real life, I like nothing more than shooting my load deep inside Matt's tight, round arse or, for the sake of variety, in his hot, wet mouth. In film, though, the lack of visible cum makes it seem that the action wasn't as hot as it seemed. It's not enough to cum, you've got to be seen to cum. Punters like to see the evidence— they want to see spunk squirt across their screens, they want to see bucket loads of it. It isn't always easy to cum on demand. Sometimes, you've been fucking for hours, sometimes you might have cum three or four times, or you just might not fancy the guy.

So, no matter how turned-on James was (and I could see that he was feeling pretty hot) he couldn't cum until the director told him to, until the director had the shot properly framed and focussed.

He was doing a good job. He hung onto Matt's hips and humped his arse hard. The sight of his magnified cock on the monitor pumping in and out of my lover's arsehole nearly made me spunk on the spot. But I was a professional—I was a stunt dick now—and I managed to hang on. Gripping my cock hard at the base, I just about satisfied my urge to stimulate myself without indulging in a full-blown wank. James was on the short strokes now, panting and grunting from the exertion and the excitement.

Matt's cock was as hard as granite—pressing flat against his muscular belly. His fist wrapped round it and began to pump it in rhythm with James's thrusts. Still clinging to my cock, I used my other hand to squeeze my balls, sending a delicious shiver of pleasure through my groin. Flesh slapped against flesh, Matt's hand was a blur as he beat his meat. James was moving quicker now, his strokes fast but shallow. Matt raised his head, his eyes wide and unseeing, and went rigid. James shuddered and almost collapsed onto Matt's back. His buttocks contracted as he dumped his load into the tip of the condom, deep inside Matt's tight hole.

"I'm sorry," he gasped apologetically. "When he started spasming, it took me by surprise, I just couldn't help it." He collapsed onto the bed beside Matt, who gave him a reassuring pat on the shoulder.

"No problem," said the director. "We'll get Jack to take your place."

I joined Matt on the bed and waited while the crew made sure that Matt and I were in the right positions. I rolled a condom onto my stiff knob and penetrated him. He pushed down against my invading cock and quickly I was firmly embedded in his gorgeous, hot hole. I wiggled when I was all the way in, rubbing my pubes against his cheeks.

I gripped his hips hard and started to slide in and out of his delicious arse. I knew it wasn't going to take long before I shot, so I made the most of the feeling. Matt's bum was like wet velvet against my prick. His sphincter muscles contracted and relaxed, providing an erotic massage as I began to ride him hard. It was almost as if his arse was trying to milk the spunk out of me. It was more than just fucking him—it felt as though his hole was sucking my cock—gripping and then yielding as I reamed him.

Matt and I were lost in a reality of our own. We were in a brightly lit, dusty warehouse in front of dozens of sweaty men pointing cameras at us; but, as far as we were concerned, we were alone. My cock and his arse were all that existed. My cock in his arse was my only thought, my only feeling, my only reality. The back of his legs were damp with sweat, where my thighs were slapping against him. I could smell his musky, sweet scent rising from his body. His hand slid up and down his straining dick, in rhythm with my thrusts. His breathing was ragged and shallow. He moaned softly.

Heat gathered in my bollocks, beginning to spread through my belly. I was on the edge. I knew that I should pull out so that we could get the cum shot on film, but I wanted to prolong this incredible sensation as long as I could. I grasped Matt's hips harder and fucked him for all I was worth. I figured I'd get maybe six strokes before I had to pull out.

One, two—I was nearly there. Three, four—this was incredible. Five—I pulled out, ripped off the condom and my cock exploded.

Spunk erupted all over the bed, arcing high over Matt's back and landing in his black hair. I threw my head back and howled. I was never going to stop cuming—stream after stream of jizz cannoned out of my cock, covering Matt and the bed.

When I finally stopped coming I fell onto the bed—I didn't have much choice, my legs wouldn't hold me up any more. Matt turned to face me and knelt in front of me—his rigid prick only inches from my face. He bent down and gave me a tender kiss on the mouth before gripping his cock and giving it a couple of quick strokes. I heard him make the cute little hissing noise. I kept my eyes trained on his groin and saw his thighs start to tremble. He grunted repeatedly as he shot his wad right into my face. The milky spunk felt warm against my skin and I caught as much as I could in my mouth as he continued to pump out jizz. I sucked the spilled seed from his softening cock.

"Cut!" the director yelled.

So there you have it—the confession of a stunt cock. It's not all fun—most of the time it strains my self-control to the limit, but I think I've found my vocation at last. Matt just loves to be watched and I just love to do the watching. Together we make an unbeatable team.

You might think that fucking all day would turn the pastime into something of a chore. I'm happy to report that this isn't the case. Horny as it is, what we do between 9 and 5 is strictly work. We still do it like bunnies in our free time. Well, you've got to do something to relax—and all work and no play makes Jack a dull boy.

The Life Saver

George Dibbs

I'D JUST MADE MY ROUNDS AND HAD GOTTEN BACK TO MY STATION. IT was mostly families on the beach today and parents were keeping tighter controls on their kids than they did at home. It was peaceful as hell.

I got comfortable in my chair at the top of the lifeguard's stand and gazed out over the blue expanse of the Gulf of Mexico below Mobile. I loved the feeling of the sun and salt air on my nearly-naked body. I loved being horny all the time and that was what my job did for me. The knob of my dick began to slowly push through the loose skin of my lace and spread across the front of my speedos.

I was thinking about him again. Vic Throttle, the star of *True Tool*. I hadn't been able to get him out of my head since I bought the video a week ago. I was only half-hard and that was where I liked to be— my dick alive enough to feel even the breeze but still soft enough so it wouldn't be embarrassing if there was trouble I had to take care of.

I forced my thoughts from Vic and admitted to myself again, like I had a lot of times before, that I had the perfect job for me. I had the perfect life even. I was twenty, tall, blond, smooth; and I had a couple of friends who got off on my looks and what I had in my Speedos. When I needed them. Three or four times a week, a hunky stranger from the beach would also want to worship me at close range— privately. In the past year and a half, I had had more ass and mouth than I could shake a stick at. All because I was a lifeguard and could parade around in just my Speedos all day. Life was way cool for Danny Grover, even if I was constantly hot for Vic Throttle this past week.

From late spring to early September, I was a lifeguard, watching the waves and surf from the Gulf of Mexico roll in. Through the winter months along the shore, I served as both caretaker and environmentalist for this same beach and the adjacent campground.

The environmental part of my job was to take water samples and turn them in to the Sea Lab located a few miles away. I also kept my eyes open for any fish kills, any debris or oil slicks, or any dolphins that seemed to be trying to beach themselves. When any of that happened, I called the marine biologist and, together, we brought in any wounded or sick sea creatures or tried to determine the source of the oil or debris coming in.

I soon was thinking again about the video I'd bought the week before. Shit! I wasn't even looking at the hunks, thinking about the thing. It was just so damned hot. I'd gone home the past five days not even thinking of my buddies I could invite over. I sure hoped I didn't wear the video out because I was playing it every night.

My dick started to get harder just at the thought of Vic Throttle's pole. If I ever did bend over and become a pincushion for anybody it would be for him. That Throttle boy had the biggest, thickest piece of meat I'd ever seen and it got me thinking of what it'd feel like in my butt every time I saw it.

As my cock lurched foreword, I realized it wasn't too soft any more. If I sat around and dreamed about Vic Throttle any longer I was going to have a full eight inch hard-on to hide if I had to help somebody out of trouble. I climbed down from my perch and started to patrol my territory.

I came up on a guy, only slightly older than myself, spreading his towel. I noticed right off that he had on a bathing suit that was a different style than what people wore on the Alabama beaches. It reminded me of some kind of rope rolled up and stretched around him just enough to cover the good parts, only it was real soft-looking—like silk. It didn't leave much to the imagination either. I figured right then that he was from some flashier place, like maybe California. I grinned as I came up even with him, and the guy nodded. His whole manner seemed downright alien. The beach towel, the shades—even his hair was cut differently than anything anyone along the Gulf Coast usually wore.

"You here by yourself?" I asked, giving him my friendliest drawl and stopping beside him.

He nodded. He removed his shades and I actually saw his face for the first time.

I gasped. "Hey, I know you from someplace!" My pulse rate shot up like a deep-space probe from Canaveral. This guy with the good looks and the great build seemed so familiar. I couldn't place him for the life of me. My dick was sending me signals, and I was a little afraid I might pop right out of my Speedos.

The guy smiled back. "You might have seen my face—or something." His tone was warm and friendly.

There was a real comfortable casualness to him that I liked. It was almost as if I'd known him for years. "Have you been in the paper or something?"

His smile widened. "Not really. I've been in some movies—videos actually. My real name is Mike, but I act under the name Vic Throttle."

My eyes bulged and my jaw just sort of dropped. This was the guy in the video! This was the guy I had beat my meat to for the past week. My dick surged so hard it was about to bust out of my Speedos. I instantly got a real itch way up my butt.

"God! Man, you're great! You really are. I have a video you're in. Wow! Who'd ever have thought I would get to meet Vic Throttle?"

"Just call me Mike, " the guy replied. "I get a little tired of my stage name. I didn't even pick it. The director on my first assignment chose it and it just stuck."

I could feel that my dick was sticky and oozing inside my Speedos. I guessed my eyes were showing everything I was feeling—like how much I wanted to see him naked, how much I wanted to feel every bit of him, and how much I wanted to lose my virginity to him. I didn't care. I put out my hand and said: "My name's Danny. Pleased to meet you."

Mike shook my hand and his eyes never left mine. He didn't stop smiling either. "You're a good guy, Danny," he said, and carefully placed the palm of his hand on my shoulder.

My eyes glazed for a second, and my breath began to come in

short, wracking sobs, like when I was shooting my load. I figured Mike could feel me struggling to stay calm. I sort of hoped he did and would get some ideas from it.

"Thanks, Mike. Man, I have really thought about you a lot—" I said, and then realized what I was admitting. "I mean, I've seen your video a lot, the one called *True Tool.*"

The sun had moved lower in the western sky, and a light breeze was playing around the edges of the waves and over the ridges of the sand. Most people had left for the next-door camp grounds or wherever their families were spending the night. Even the seagulls had begun to slow down their relentless shrieks.

I turned to Mike. "It's about time for me to check out at the lifeguard station. Then I'm going to go to the showers. You want to meet me there?" My voice was hopeful.

Maybe Mike was touched. Maybe he was horny. Maybe, coming from the West Coast where I'd heard that too much was fake, he felt a warmth toward this guileless lifeguard. I didn't know why he decided to let me tag along with him, but I was glad he did. I was in lust.

"Sure." He shrugged. "I've got my things in one of those lockers anyway."

When I'd put up my sign at the stand and gotten my things I headed directly for the showers. I didn't know what to expect and I was afraid to expect much. But I was sure hoping Mike would invite me to wherever he was staying. I had a bone that was harder than any that I could remember.

There wasn't anyone in the showers or among the lockers except Mike. He was sitting on a bench watching the door. He grinned when I walked in and I saw that friendly grin become sex-charged when he saw that my dick was hard. I wondered what the etiquette was for being alone, nearly naked, with your eight, thick inches hard as a rock in front of a pornstar you were praying to get into something with.

Mike began pulling off his strange swimsuit. I stood beside the lockers watching him and wanting to see his dick for real, all ten inches of it. Him for real—in the flesh. I made no effort to hide my erection. Jesus! I wanted him to notice it. I wanted him to want me.

"Hey, man, you look just like you do in your videos," I told him, my eyes glued to his smooth chest and tight six-pack. I absent-mindedly pulled on my dick through my Speedos.

Mike finished stripping and walked over to me. He put his hand on my shoulders and smiled at me. "I look like I do in the videos because I am in those videos."

I blushed as I grinned back and said: "Oh yeah... I forgot."

Mike chuckled. "You must have something on your mind, forgetting something like that."

I reached over and took his meat in my hand. I didn't grip it or anything—just let it lay across my open palm. My whole attention was on his thing. "Something like that," I managed to say.

We began our showers side by side. I saw him giving me a real close look and I hoped that he was seeing that I was no gym queen, that I was the real thing. I hoped he didn't mind that I was uncut now that he was seeing my dick naked and in the light. I didn't want a repeat of what had happened with that Yankee boy at the beginning of summer. We'd been feeling each other up hot and heavy on my couch until we moved into a sixty-nine position and he felt my extra skin. After that, I could suck him but my dick wasn't going close to his face because he thought it was unclean. He wouldn't even let me pork him, even with a rubber on. I wanted all of Mike, any way he'd give himself to me. Only, I didn't want him thinking I was dirty or something.

I jumped when I felt Mike's fingers wrap around my bone and pull the skin along the shaft. He teased the ridge of the helmet with his fingernail and my knees nearly gave out under me. I gripped the nozzle pipe for support.

His other hand spread across the slope of my ass, feeling that slope and the firmness of my butt cheeks. "Nice," he mumbled against my ear.

"Hmmmm," I moaned and pressed my fanny back against his hand, liking the feel of having him so close to my virginity. His lips found mine.

He pushed my butt forward slightly and my dick pushed against his fist. His thumb rubbed the exposed expanse of my knob and that had me pulling away from the stimulation, right back into his hand spread across my butt and pushing me forward again. His middle finger found my crack and went exploring.

I was into it, the slow, sensuous movement of me fucking his hand, warm water pouring down on me. His finger found my hole and began to make ever smaller circles around the wrinkled skin guarding my rear entrance. It slipped into me and I was ready to climb the water pipes as new sensations spread up over my body. My balls tightened and I realized I was almost at the point of no return.

"No, Mike," I groaned, pulling away from his tongue and lips despite not wanting things to change at all. But they had to if I was going to have any chance of getting into something with him. I didn't want a hand job and a goodbye kiss; I wanted him.

"What's the matter, Danny?"

"I want—" I looked down to his fist on my pole. "I want to suck you off. I want you to fuck me—in a bed."

Mike laughed. "Let's dry off and get dressed. I've got a king sized bed at the motel and a box of rubbers." He kissed my cheek. "I've even got lube."

Mike kept the lights dimmed way down as we entered his room. It sort of relaxed me, making me feel like I was making the right decision—even though there never had been a decision for me. I was Mike's the moment he took off his sunglasses and looked at me on the beach.

Closing the door behind us, Mike reached out and took my shoulders in his hands. I leaned back against him as his fingers moved down the front of my shirt, one button at a time. His lips traced my jaw and moved down my neck onto my shoulders as I relaxed against him. I finally understood what the guys I'd picked up had felt like as we moved toward me fucking them. I only hoped I'd made them feel as good about it as Mike was making me feel. My dick was waiting to leap out as soon as my boxers were dropped. The itch up my ass was just as demanding.

When we were both stripped naked, I began running my lips and my tongue all over Mike's body, while he just stood there, letting me explore him to my heart's content.

My bone was bouncing as I worked, precum beginning to drip.

My dick quivered, wanting to be touched. Mike reached down while I was sucking on his nipples and gave my meat a friendly tug. I gasped and my pole began to spasm as it thickened even more. Suddenly I was shooting load after load, cum spewing out in thick, white, rope-like strands. I held on to Mike and gasped for breath.

"You are one hot dude," he whispered against my ear. He moved me to the side of the bed and, holding me, laid me down on the bed. "Just lay on your back and let me take charge."

I nodded, my eyes almost glazing as I watched Mike open a rubber and spread it across the head of his dick, then slowly down onto its shaft. That was the dick I'd been wanting for a week. The dick I wanted enough to give up being a top. It was perfect—long, thick, hard. He lifted my legs and put my thighs onto my chest. I was exposed, my crack spread wide open and opening the crevice into my hole.

My eyes followed his dick as it came to me. As its wide head pressed against my pucker. As it slid into me. I knew enough to push down to open myself up enough to take it. I still groaned as that knob shredded my sphincter and pushed into virgin territory. "Give me a minute," I told him.

"Does it hurt?" He stopped and looked down into my face, searching it, and I didn't know what he wanted to find.

"No. I just need to get used to it being there is all."

His eyes widened with understanding. "You're a virgin?"

"I was." I grinned up at him. "But I don't think I can ever say that again—not now." I took a deep breath. "Okay, give me some more of that monster."

I concentrated on opening myself up as Mike eased his dick deeper and further into me. I sighed as his pubes finally scratched the bottom of my ballsac and I knew he was all the way in.

"For a virgin, you took that like a pro," he chuckled and got up on his knees. I crossed my ankles behind his neck to keep my ass elevated enough that my butthole was level with his dick.

"I've had a week of watching those boys in *True Tool* adjust to you going into them."

He grinned and ground his dick around in me, really massaging my love nut. My dick went all the way hard and drooled in apprecia-tion. "Fuck me, Mike," I told him.

I could feel the slight touch of the air circulating in the room as it caressed the hairs on my legs. The slow, steady movement of his dick in my ass. My dick was more sensitive than it ever had been before. My nipples tightened and I couldn't believe what the air was doing to them. I was staying close. My whole body became a receptacle for Mike as he fucked me.

"It's so good," I moaned in appreciation and ground my butt against his forward thrust. I beat my meat in time to his movement in me. And I never wanted our sex to end. He was picking up speed, however, and, as his warhead started to bash my love nut hard and fast, my eyes opened double wide. "God, man, that's great!"

"Here I come!" Mike growled as he started giving me short, explosive thrusts. I started pumping my dick hard to catch up with him. My first rope was rushing up my cumtube when he slammed into my ass with all ten of his inches and held there. His dick grew inside me and I felt his shot hit the rubber at the same time mine was flying over my head, hitting me in the face, and finally puddling on my stomach.

We held on to each other for a long time. Not saying anything, just savoring the completeness of the moment and our union.

In the morning, I got up to head back to the beach. I felt better than I could ever remember. I looked down at Mike who was just beginning to rouse.

Well, this was it, I told myself, letting myself feel a little let down. I was going to work and Mike was going back to California. At least I would have the video to play anytime I wanted to remind myself of Mike.

"Where are you going?" Mike asked sleepily.

"Gotta go to work, man. Got a job to do." I pulled my eyes away from him; they'd suddenly become misty. I didn't want to think I was a teary-eyed deflowered virgin. I was just as much a man as he was, even if I sniffed and had to wipe my eyes.

"Can you call somebody to substitute for you?"

"Yeah," I answered dubiously. "Why?"

He sat up and grabbed my arm. Pulling me around to face him, he said: "I want you to come back to California with me."

I couldn't believe it. I just stood there, trying to take it all in.

"Me? You want me to go out there with you?"

"Sure. You're a natural, Danny. The video industry hasn't seen anyone like you in years. You'll be a star."

I understood what he was saying; after all, my mama hadn't raised a dummy. I felt like a steam roller had rolled over me and I didn't know if it had felt good or not. "Could I stay with you?" I asked slowly.

"Stay? Hell, Danny, you better be sleeping in the same bed with me—every night."

I smiled. I liked the idea of that. I liked it a whole lot.

Dances With Coyote

Bryan Nakai

I COULDN'T BELIEVE THIS WAS HAPPENING TO ME. WHY HAD I LISTENED to that asshole photographer of mine, and rented a car? Mais oui, I had seen plenty of the Beautiful American Desert—red dust, parched stone, mummified plant skeletons. I could have been ten thousand feet above this oven, relaxing in first class with a glass of wine. Instead, I simmered in my own sweat, waiting for a damned tow truck.

I wiped another gallon or so of sweat from my face. Surely the mechanic would arrive at any moment. The damned car phone battery refused to power another call. I moved to the dubious shelter of some crumbling rocks beside the road. The car must be hot enough to bake croissants in by now. Not that it was that much cooler outside; I just had the advantage of the occasional hot breeze to stir my sweat-stained clothing.

An odd rumbling, sliding noise behind me made my hair stand on end. Earthquake?

I ran to crouch behind the car, expecting to see the entire side of the red hill tumble down upon me. Instead, a small herd of ponies thundered over it, parting to gallop around the car. Behind them, sweat glistening on their naked chests, rode four Indians.

Real Red Indians, I was sure. Savages! Well, they did have on boots and blue jeans, but their long black hair and bronzed skin left no doubt that they were Indians. I had never seen any before. I guessed they had probably stolen the horses from some farmer and wondered if he survived still.

I wished I had never come to America. After this, any boy who wanted to be in a J.P. Gamipole film could fly to me for the next casting session!

I swallowed, wiping suddenly clammy palms onto my khaki trousers. I tried to remember which reservation I'd been driving across, and whether the tribes within it were hostile. All I could remember was the American cowboy movie I had seen last month, where the settlers were massacred.

Three of the men pulled their ponies to a stop, looking down on me with broad, impassive faces. The fourth continued after the herd. I stood slowly, hoping I had not provoked them.

"I come in peace," I said loudly.

The three looked at each other. "Piss?" one of them asked in a deep voice. I noticed he had a body I would want anytime in any of my videos. Another muttered something guttural, doubtless in their native tongue. I decided to try again.

Pointing to my chest, I introduced myself. "Jean Paul Gamipole. I mean you no harm."

The smallest Indian swung lithely from his pony, striding towards me with a purposeful walk that reminded me of a man wading through knee-deep water. I swallowed the dust in my throat as he pushed past me. He poked his head into the window of the wretched Cadillac and grunted something in that singsong language. I thought I heard a chuckle from one of the others, but when I glanced up, their faces were as impassive as ever. The Indian waded back to stand in front of me.

"You rich man?" he grunted, fingering the lapels of my silk shirt. I nodded hurriedly, remembering some words of their language from the movie.

"I have plenty wampum. You fix car, I give you many horses."

One of the two still on horseback grunted something, and the one before me nodded. He swung back astride his mount and kicked it to a gallop. I shaded my eyes to watch him catch up to the herd. These savages were graceful; I had to admit that. The other two sat silently, until their companion returned leading a spotted pony. Immediately they were off their mounts and had closed in upon me, hoisting me from the ground by my elbows.

"Mon Dieu!" I groaned as my feet left the dusty earth. "Do not scalp me—my people will make war upon you!"

My captors threw me across the pony, and I clenched my hands in its coarse mane as we galloped across the desert after the herd. I also clenched my jaw, to keep from biting my tongue, as the pony tossed me from one end of its dusty back to the other. My ass was numb when we finally stopped, and the Indians had to haul me off the pony. My knees buckled.

Three of my captors dragged me to a rounded, earthen hut. The fourth again remained with the horses, herding them into a corral beside the hut. I blinked helplessly in the darkness, afraid to take a step. One of the braves jerked me toward the left, where I collapsed against the surprising coolness of the dirt wall. I heard the flare of a match, then the darkness receded as a kerosene lantern glowed from its hook amid the rafters.

The hut didn't look lived in. The walls were festooned with the accoutrements necessary for riding—saddles, bridles, ambiguous leather straps and buckles. Bales of hay took up nearly half the large room, stacked higher than my head and making my nose wrinkle with their dusty smell. A faded woolen rug covered the floor.

The Indian at my elbow muttered something to his friends in his deep voice, then squatted before me. I looked away from his expressionless bronze face and guessed he was the leader of his band. My gaze dipped over broad shoulders, a wide, smooth chest glistening in the lamplight, and slender hips clad in worn denim. Had I not been in such peril, I would have been trying to hire him for my next picture.

"You not American," my deep-voiced captor grunted. "What you do on Navajo reservation?"

I tried to clear the dust from my throat. "I am from France. Far across big ocean. I make the movies."

"Z movies?" the Indian across the room muttered, scratching his head.

The other savages grunted. One of them said something in what I now supposed was Navajo, and ducked through the doorway. "Maybe you think you make Navajo movie?" the deep-voiced leader before me growled. His fingers closed on my shirtfront, and he suddenly jerked me to my feet. "Navajo not make *Dances With Wolves*."

"No!" I squeaked, cringing. "I not make the serious film. I make the naughty film!"

Both men looked at me blankly, then glanced at one another.

"Naughty feem?" the one holding my lapels asked. "What means 'naughty feem'?"

I flinched. I knew they were making jokes because of my accent. But I was here, alone, with savages—and who knew what attitude they had toward gay erotic cinema? I cleared my throat.

"I make the movie where men... er... make love."

The braves exchanged another glance.

"You gay film director?" the leader demanded. I nodded, praying they didn't have an automatic death penalty for such things.

The Indians stood in silence for a moment, staring at one another. I had the impression they were in shock. The one holding me cleared his throat loudly and released me. The other brave coughed. They headed for the doorway.

"Stay," the leader ordered me. I had no inclination to disobey.

After a few minutes, three of them stepped back inside. The third brave was wiping his eyes with a huge bandanna.

"We decide we not believe you," the leader one said, clearing his throat. "Prove you gay film director."

I sagged against the wall. How could I prove that, with no modern technology in sight? It wasn't as though I routinely traveled with a VCR and sample tapes, after all.

"I—" I tried to think of some plausible excuse. The wide chested leader strode back to grab my shirt again. I opened my mouth to scream, then realized that his strong fingers were unbuttoning it.

"Want demonstration," he grunted, tugging my shirt down around my waist. I got the point. I'd come to America in search of new talent—now I had to prove my own. This was a twisted casting couch scene, with God-only-knew-what consequences should I fail my "screen test." Swallowing hard, I wriggled out of the shirt, folding it neatly on a hay bale in case my captors decided to release me. I could only pray they would be satisfied with a strip show.

The two other braves stepped closer to watch the show. I worked my trousers slowly down my legs, trying to keep my knees from knocking together. My hands trembled, and I had to force myself not to cover my wilted cock. My balls were trying to crawl back inside my body. I had gooseflesh on my gooseflesh. I wondered if any of my film stars in Paris had ever been this nervous on a casting couch.

The Indians crowded around to run their hands across my trembling chest. Bronze fingers slid through my chest hair, tugged at my nipples. Despite my fear, my nubs soon hardened, standing straight out as though begging for more attention. The musky odor of sweat rose from the bodies around me—sweat and horse and old leather. I inhaled deeply, and felt a tingle beginning deep within my groin.

A dark head dipped downward; I felt hot breath on one nipple. My chest arched outward as a strong tongue flicked back and forth. My fingers clenched around someone's belt, someone's broad hands pulled me to lean against a smooth chest. Thick, calloused fingers caressed my hair. A fist closed over my cock.

"Paleface put on good show," the leader growled in my ear. "Maybe we let him go after."

"What do you want?" I squeaked. In response, the hands on my body tugged downwards, until the four of us sprawled across the thick woolen rug. I could hardly catch my breath; my heart thudded in my throat.

The leader wriggled out of his trousers. His long, thick, dark cock was already hard, standing nearly straight out from the thick, black pubes. To my relief, one of the others tossed a box of condoms in our direction. The leader ripped open one packet, rolling the latex over his shaft.

I opened my mouth almost without thinking. He smelled of sweat and leather. I choked a bit as he thrust forward. He pulled away to let me catch my breath, then began a slow, steady rhythm, with my throat the sheath for his blade. I ran my hands over his glistening body, sliding my fingers over his asscheeks. The heavy muscles bunched under my hands as he thrust into my mouth.

Calloused hands supported me, tugging at my nipples, my balls. Someone fisted my cock again. This time, it responded, throbbing into hardness under the rough hand. The cock in my throat swelled, thrusting deeper. I could feel the body above me tense, ready to shoot a load of cream into my mouth. I squeezed his ass, pulling him inside me. With a groan, he clenched his fingers in my hair, pumping my throat as his hot load burst forth. I struggled to breathe as his thickened cock filled the condom with cream. His hands held my head firmly against him, keeping my mouth where he wanted it. I could only writhe in his grasp, struggling against the muscular bodies around me.

At last, he gave a final, quivering thrust, and withdrew. I gasped for air, collapsing onto the floor like a wet rag. I barely had the energy to groan as a second cock, already sheathed in latex, pressed against my lips. This was at least a more comfortable size than the first, and I managed to satisfy the second brave without too much difficulty. I had hopes that they would be content to use my mouth, rather than stretching my poor asshole. It had been a long time since I bottomed in the boudoir.

I had barely closed my lips over the final, glistening cock, when I felt fingers between my legs. Every muscle in my body stiffened. I could feel my cock wilting. The third brave pulled away from my lips, squatting to watch the action.

"White man have tight hole," the one behind me grunted, shoving a finger roughly inside. I recognized his voice; he had been the big one who took my mouth first, the leader.

"White man not bottom in long time," I gasped, squirming as he slid a second finger beside the first.

"Good. You learn something maybe," he answered.

Something cold and slippery dribbled over my ass, and I gasped. I realized that the well-equipped leader had somehow located a tube of lubricant—perhaps they'd riffled my suitcase. At least they didn't seem to be want to harm me. I couldn't keep myself from quivering, though, as those fingers greased my pucker. A glance behind me and I saw my captor's other hand rolling a condom over his thick shaft. When I felt the hard knob of his cock, I sucked in a deep breath and closed my eyes.

The thick pole speared past my tight hole, stretching me wider than I thought I could take. I moaned at the stab of pain.

He thrust slowly inside, then paused, waiting while my throbbing ass grew accustomed to the intrusion. I could hear my own panting breath as my captors stared silently down at me. Their thick fingers slid across the sweat on my chest, tugged once more at my nipples.

I trembled beneath their touch. The cock up my ass was one any of my video stars would have been proud to display for the camera—long and wide, and straight as the proverbial arrow. At that moment, I would have appreciated it better shoved up someone else's hole.

I slowly grew accustomed to the massive shaft impaling me. The leader felt my muscles relax, and pulled slowly back. I whimpered as he withdrew nearly the entire length, then slowly—oh, so slowly!—filled my hole once more. As he began pumping my ass, I forgot about the other hands on my body. I was only aware of his cock, stretching me wide, filling me completely. And how good it felt.

His broad hands held my hips in place—strong hands, calloused from work. I wanted those hands on my body, wanted this man. I shoved backwards to meet his thrusts, grunting with desire.

A hand lifted my chin. For a moment, I could not focus—my entire mind seemed centered on my ass. Then, I understood what the Indian wanted. I opened my mouth and he slipped his cock inside.

Impaled at both ends, I lost my fears. I sucked hungrily at the cock within my throat, eager for more internal massage. This one was nowhere near the size of the monster stretching my ass, but it filled my mouth nicely. The Indian beside me suddenly slid his hand between my legs, roughly fisting my cock.

The brave at my head held me tightly against his pubes as he thrust his shaft down my throat. My hips were welded to the Indian impaling me from behind, and now an iron fist clenched my cock. I could only whimper, wishing for climax as sensation after sensation washed over me—and wishing for this never to end.

The cock within my mouth swelled, ready to release its hot load. I choked as the brave pulled my face to his groin, pumping wildly. My body quivered helplessly in his grasp. Then, I felt the first load of cream fill the condom, burning my throat. I struggled to breathe as a second eruption quickly followed the first, swelling the mass within me. The Indian thrust hard within my throat, groaning loudly, then withdrew.

The leader behind me still kept up a furious rhythm in my ass. I could feel the deep pounding that meant he was nearing climax. His fingers dug into my sides. "Prends-moi!" I begged him. "Take me!"

"Fuck!" he yelled, shoving forward. The massive cock seemed to swell even wider as it emptied itself into my demanding ass. Molten jets of cream seared my canal, so much that I feared he would burst the condom.

The fist around my cock pumped mercilessly as I writhed in my captor's grasp. I felt my own climax boiling up. A final burst of hot cream shot into my ass, and my balls erupted. The Indian behind me continued to pump my ass, wringing more cream from my cock than I'd ever thought possible. The room began to spin around me.

I only faded out for a moment. When I could think once more, I found myself on my back, with one of my captors on either side of me. Their hands continued to stroke my chest. I realized that I had done more than pass a casting couch session—I had learned something about my desires.

I rolled toward my massive brave. Our lips met. I opened my mouth, wanting to taste this savage man. Our tongues met and wrestled with the strength of our longing. My hands roamed his smooth, hard chest, sliding through the sheen of sweat that covered us both.

I felt hands sliding along my ass, and spread my legs for the man behind me. My ass felt empty. I sighed happily as two fingers slipped inside.

"I guess you are a porn director," the leader murmured beside me. "That was the best fuck I've had."

My eyes flew open. I stared into the chocolate brown eyes of the man who'd fulfilled a desire I hadn't known I possessed. They crinkled with laughter. I pulled my lips away.

"You speak the English!" I shouted indignantly.

"A hell of a lot better than you do," muttered the brave behind me, his fingers still massaging my prostate.

"I'm sorry," the man in my arms said, his lips quirking as he tried not to laugh. "I guess Coyote got to me. But you were so damned funny!"

"All those lines from B-movies," his companion added. "Or were they Z movies?"

I could only stare helplessly. The million questions buzzing inside my head resolved into one. "Coyote?"

The wide lips brushed against mine in a quick kiss. "My people believe that Coyote is the mischief maker, the one who brings chaos."

My head whirled. "And you let me think that you were—?"

"Dumb savages," he finished. "You seemed to expect it."

My face flushed. "I never met a real Indian before," I mumbled.

"Maybe now you won't be so quick to assume," he said, waving a thick finger at me. "I hope you've learned your lesson."

His finger teased my lips. I sucked it inside, staring into his dark eyes. I had learned many things, yes. The deep rumble of a motor sounded from outside, rapidly approaching.

"I guess Eddie put some gas in your car," the second brave announced, pulling his fingers from inside me. I sighed, wanting them back. "We probably ought to head back to the ranch pretty soon."

My fingers tightened on the brawny arms holding me. Dark eyes looked down into mine, expressionless over high bronze cheekbones. "I wish to have the dance with that Coyote one more time before I leave," I whispered, slipping my hand between his thighs to grasp the already thickening shaft.

"Tu vieux monter dans ma maison?" he whispered.

I stared up in surprise, unable to breathe. "Of course I want to go home with you! How is it that you speak the French as well?"

White teeth flashed in a wide grin, startling against that dark face. "I had to take a year of foreign language in college," he replied. "I thought French was romantic."

"Cheri, let me show you how romantic the French can be!" I told him and pulled him to me. His lips met mine as the Indian behind me pushed into my welcoming hole.

Made Man

Simon Sheppard

"HE'S FAMILY."

"Well, of course he's family."

"No, he's... Family."

"Gay? You've got a gay father? That's cool!"

"No, I mean he's the kind of man you wouldn't want to cross because—" Vin's eyes narrowed significantly. "He's got friends, y'know? Friends you wouldn't want to fuck with."

Leo gulped. "Mafia? Your father's Mafia?

"Uh, they don't call themselves that any more." Vin was pulling off his tight T-shirt. His nipples were prominent on his lean, shaved chest. Leo couldn't help but notice.

"Well, this role," the casting director said, "will take some acting as well as a big dick."

"A big dick, I've got," Vin smiled, a smile as warm as an ice dildo. "And I bet I've got that part, too—if my father has anything to say about it." He stood before Leo's desk, hips thrust forward, and unbuckled his belt. He pulled the leather belt free in one smooth motion, twirled it around his head like he was a stripper, and let it fly into a corner of the office.

"Sure, sure, you're in the running, but it's an important part in a big video, our biggest budget yet, and you're—uh—not a name."

"Not yet," Vin said, unbuttoning his fly, "but wait till those wankers get a load of this." And sure enough, the bulge in his gray cotton briefs was sizable.

Oh my God, Leo thought, I'm sitting here while a wise guy's son shows me his dick. It sprang forth, half-hard, as Vin peeled down his briefs.

"Listen, Vin, I don't know what you heard, but there's no place for the mob at this company, none at all."

"Yeah," said Vin with an evil grin, "but there's a place for me in *Studmen*. The starring role. If you know what's good for you."

Arching from well-trimmed, blue-black pubic hair, his uncut dick was darkish tan, with a big pink head. As he stroked his meat, peeling back the foreskin, it grew to fill his paw.

"Okay, that's fine, Vin. Only it's not just my decision to make. There's the producer, the director... We'll get back to you, you can meet with the other guys involved—"

As Leo spoke, Vin kind of shuffled around the desk, jeans down around his knees, till his crotch was right in Leo's face.

"Want to suck it, man? Go on, take a taste."

Leo could smell Vin's sweat, and the odor went straight to his crotch. "No, that's really not necessary. There's no casting couch here at Redhot Videos."

"I said, SUCK IT, motherfucker. You wouldn't want my daddy mad at you, would you, Mr. DeAngelis?" He slapped his hard-on across Leo's cheek.

"Um... yeah, okay." Leo opened wide. It was going to be a mouthful. As the head slid between his lips, he flashed on Marlon Brando and his orange-rind teeth. An offer he couldn't refuse.

As the cockflesh slid across his tongue, he tried to figure a way out of this. He and his partners had already decided that Kris would be offered the part; if they had a superstar at Redhot, Kris was it. His face on the box sold copies. Dildos were modeled on his dick (with an extra inch or two thrown in for good measure). Hell, he could almost act, even. And Kris had let it be known that once the year was up, he was thinking of accepting an exclusive contract with Barry Stein and those slimeballs over at Hotrod Films.

But if Kris starred in *Studmen* what was he going to tell the mobster? "Sorry, Mr. Stroker, but your son didn't get the part. Now please have your goons break both my legs." Yeah, that'd work. That'd work real good.

"You like that, Leo? You like that big dick?"

Well, he did like it, rather, though the size of it threatened to make him gag. As did the porn-cliché dialogue. But, if the porn connoisseurs who bought Redhot tapes could ignore clunky scripts, so could Leo.

Vin was plowing Leo's throat so hard he sputtered. He grabbed hold of Vin's muscular thighs and pushed him away.

"Okay," Leo said, "you've made your point." He found himself, despite his better instincts, rubbing his palms over the young man's smooth, defined pecs. God, the kid did have a nice body. Nicer than Kris's, if it came to that.

"So I get the fuckin' part?"

"We'll... we'll see."

"Not good enough, Leo."

DeAngelis tried to imagine what it would be like to wake up with a horse's head in his bed. Or just to wake up dead. He thought fast, as fast as he could.

"Okay, okay, Vin. You got it." He hoped that God would forgive him for lying about porn contracts. "I'll get the forms printed up and you can stop by tomorrow morning to sign."

"Really?"

"Yeah, really." It was less convincing than Leo might have hoped. But Vin had backed off, and was pulling up his pants, up to his balls, so his mostly-hard cock was hanging over the edge of his briefs.

"You better not be shitting me." As he said it, he was stroking his cock, squeezing the shaft. The movement of foreskin over headflesh, back and forth, back and forth, damn near had Leo in a trance.

"Tomorrow at... ten, okay?"

"Don't worry, DeAngelis, I can act. And I can perform as well." A drop of precum glinted from Vin's piss-hole. "Want to see?"

Leo had to admit that Stroker had, if not exactly star quality, "something." The sight of him handling that fat piece of uncut meat was, as Siskel would have said, compelling. Or Ebert. "Yeah," said Leo DeAngelis, "show me."

Vin's stroking accelerated. He half-closed his eyes, threw his head back, arched his body. His muscular chest swelled with rapid breaths. And with a masculine little grunt, Vin Stroker shot his load. Thick, ropy gobs of cum landed on a pile of papers on the desk, on the cheap Oriental carpet, and all over Leo's khaki Dockers.

Leo wasn't sure whether he should applaud.

"Hey, bud, looks like I hit you. Sorry." Vin reached down to the khakis, swiped off a puddle of jizz, and brought his hand to his mouth, licking it clean. "Ten tomorrow it is," Stroker said, pulling on his T-shirt. That evil grin again. "I won't be late. Don't you be."

When Vin had closed the office door behind himself, Leo finally permitted himself a breath. Jesus! He had till ten tomorrow to figure something out. Or to get out of town.

The rest of the staff of Redhot Videos had taken the day off. Both of them. He hit Bryan's button on the phone. If *Studmen* had become *Goodfellas*, Bryan had a right to know. In fact, Bryan, as the producer, the head of the company, and his friend, might well have a duty to do something-or-other about it. "Hi, this is Bryan Ng. I'm either not here, on the other line, or fucking..." Leo left a call-me-back message on Bryan's machine.

After he hung up, he stared aimlessly around the office; it was silly to let this get to him. Empty threats were all they were. He noticed Vin's forgotten belt lying curled in the corner of the office, like a snake ready to strike. A trouser snake. Oh well, he'd deal with it tomorrow morning. Tomorrow morning. Jesus.

It was near quitting time. Leo busied himself with odds and ends, answering mail, trying not to think about the Kiss of Death. He'd just about calmed himself down when he opened a nasty letter from some right-wing vigilantes who called themselves ChristAlmighty. He'd gotten to the part that threatened Redhot with eternal damnation when the telephone rang.

Bryan didn't wait for a hello. "So what's so important? I was in the shower when you called."

More likely, Leo knew, he was in Mike, his hunky young assistant and the firm's third employee. "It's that Stroker kid. He came to see me today. He wants the part. His father's a made man, Bryan."

"Made by who?"

"No, a made man, a gangster, part of the mob. And this kid wants the lead in *Studmen*, or else."

"Fuck, Leo, you know that role goes to Kris. I already promised him. And we know Kris can act. Why'd you even bother seeing Stroker?"

Leo sighed heavily. "The next time you promise somebody a part, you might consider informing your casting director, Bryan. So what am I gonna do?"

"Oh, the kid's full of hot air, I bet."

"I'm not so sure. Listen, why don't we try casting him? Maybe in a smaller role or something, just to keep him happy. What's the worst that can happen? He's actually pretty talented." Leo smiled thinly, remembering the size of Stroker's schlong.

"We don't give in to blackmail, and that's that."

"Easy for you to say. You haven't been threatened with a rub-out. Yet."

"Just blow him off, Leo." Bryan's breathing had altered; Leo could picture Mike on his knees, sucking Bryan's cock while he was still on the phone. Mike believed in keeping his job.

"He's coming in tomorrow at ten." Leo stared down at the 8x10 glossy of Vin Stroker on his desk.

"Sorry, I have an important meeting in Ventura then." Uh-huh, Leo thought. "But I'm quite sure you can handle it. Blow him off. That's an order."

Leo believed in keeping his job, too. "Okay, okay, Bryan. I'll tell him no dice. Kris gets the part. I just hope we don't live to regret this. In fact, I just hope we live, period." Bryan's phone crashed noisily to the floor. There were moaning sounds, like Bryan was coming in young Mike's mouth, and then the phone was hung up with a click.

"I forgot my belt."

With a start, Leo looked up from Vin's glossy to the man himself, standing there in the office door.

"So I came back for it. We came back for it." He stepped into the room, a black leather briefcase in his hand. Two other men followed him, muscling their substantial way into Leo's office. "Leo, meet Carl and Tony, friends of my dad's. Boys, this is Leo, the schmuck who's going to give that part to someone else." The evil grin. "I heard what you said on the phone, DeAngelis."

Improbably, Leo felt himself trembling. Well, not so improbably, really. Tony and Carl looked like they didn't fuck around.

"What do you have to say for yourself now, Mr. Bigshot Casting Director?" The evil grin changed to a smirk. "Boys, looks like DeAngelis here has an appointment to audition for *us*."

Leo looked around, tense and confused. Oh, God, he thought, don't let them cut off my ear. Or anything else.

"Stand up, Mr. DeAngelis." Carl and Tony strode over to either side of the desk. They wore identical black leather jackets. Not the motorcycle kind. The mobster kind. Under other circumstances, the men would have been Leo's type—dark, rough-trade guys whose eyebrows met in the middle. Different from the perfect gym bunnies that he always cast in Redhot projects.

"Hey," Leo, said, trying for small talk, "are you guys brothers?"

"Stand up, asshole," said Tony. Or Carl.

"Didn't you hear what he said?" said Carl. Or Tony.

Leo stood.

"Let's see what he's got, Carl," said Stroker.

"Okay, boss." Carl was the taller one then, the one on the right. Carl reached into his jacket and pulled out a knife, a gravity blade job that swung open with a click and a threat. Carl grabbed Leo by the collar and, with his knife hand, sliced off Leo's shirt buttons. One. By. One. Carl had Binaca on his breath. Tony helped his maybe-brother strip off the shirt.

"The T-shirt, too, boys."

"Hey that's a Calvin—" Leo started to say; but, with a rip, the knife cut through the white cotton, the dull side of the blade cold against Leo's skin. The ripped-apart shirt hung limply from Leo's shoulders.

"Hey, Mr. Casting Director. Not hitting the gym as often as we should, huh?"

It was ridiculous under the circumstances, but Leo felt a twinge of self-consciousness about his body, especially the furry little paunch that had lately found a home at his waistline.

Tony had started undoing Leo's belt while Carl skittered the tip of the knife over Leo's torso and breathed Binaca in his face. With a zip, the Dockers were undone. They fell to Leo's ankles.

"Cute undies," Vin said. They were the Joe Boxers with the big yellow smiley face.

Carl inserted the knife into the boxers' fly, right by the smiley face's tongue, and drew it upward till it sliced clear through the elastic waistband. Smiley-face crumpled and fell to the floor.

"Get that stuff off, dickhead," Tony growled. Leo kicked off his loafers and stepped out of his khakis and what was left of his once-cheery boxer shorts.

"Now, Leo… I can call you Leo, can't I? I hear you like your pornstars all smooth and hairless. Ain't that right?"

"Yes." A dry, small response.

Vin laid his briefcase on the desk, opened it, and pulled out a razor strop, a can of shaving cream, and a pearl-handled straight-edge razor. He unfolded the blade. It looked silvery and sharp. Carl and Tony grabbed Leo by the wrists, pushed him back to the wall behind the desk, and pinned him there, arms outstretched. Vin Stroker shook up the can of shaving cream and slowly, deliberately covered Leo's torso and belly with a thick layer of lime-scented lather, making his way down to Leo's cock, which to Leo's somewhat shamefaced astonishment was more than half erect.

Stroker grinned at the sight. "Men are pigs," he said. He laid one end of the well-worn razor strop on Leo's chair, pinning it there with his boot. He stropped the straight-edge till it sliced through one of Leo's faxes like it was gliding through Crisco.

"I wouldn't fidget, if I was you," Vin said. He brought the blade down across Leo's chest. It scraped through the hair, leaving a smooth, foamless swath in its wake. Stroker reached down for the boxers, wiped the blade clean on the grinning face, and started in again. The damp, citrusy foam, the sudden breeze on his hairless skin, the keen threat of the blade—it all was more than a little exciting.

"He's still hard, boss," Carl said. "The faggot fuckface."

Vin had reached the lower belly. He shaved it clean, then started in on Leo's pubes. "One false move—" he chortled, moving down to Leo's ballsac. "If I was you, Mr. Casting Director, I'd stay really still just about now." Kneeling, Stroker did a nick-free job between Leo's legs.

If we don't make him a pornstar, Leo thought, he could always be a barber.

"Finished," said Stroker, pulling Leo's hard-on down with a thumb, then letting it go to thwack up against his belly. "Turn him around, boys."

Sweat was pouring down Leo's now-hairless torso. What were they going to do, shave the crack of his ass?

Tony and Carl got him pinned up against the wall, his hard-on scraping against the nondescript wallpaper. "He still seems to be having a good time, boys. Let's see how much he enjoys this."

Leo struggled to turn his head, glancing over his shoulder. A gun! Christ, the crazy motherfucker had a nasty little black handgun pointed straight at him! He was so scared he would've pissed in his pants, if he were wearing pants, and if he could've pissed with a hard-on.

"You can have the part, Vin," he groaned. "It's all yours."

"Too late, shithead. Too late. Now face the wall."

Leo felt the cold gun barrel moving slowly, so slowly down the middle of his back, right down his spine. Past the small of his back. Parting the cheeks of his ass. All the way to his hole. And Jesus, he was still excited. Oh well, if he was going to die, he might as well do it with a hard-on.

"You'll do just what I say, motherfucker. Not one move more, not one move less. Carl, let go of his wrist and go sit on the desk. With your dick out. Now then, shit-for-brains, turn around. Nice and slow."

Carl, his jacket and his fly open, perched on the edge of Leo's desk. Carl's cock was uncut, too, not as big as Vin's maybe, but with a nice, long foreskin. Leo let himself stare. After all, it was probably the last dick he was ever going to see.

"Now bend over, nice and slow, and take that straight man's pussy-fucking dick in your faggot mouth."

As Leo bent over, his buttcheeks parted; the muzzle of the gun pressed in on his hole. He opened wide and gulped down Carl's cock, which eagerly swelled to fill his mouth. Jesus, what was that his crotch smelled like? Aramis? Binaca and Aramis. Christ.

"You be sure to do a good job," Tony said. "He doin' a good job,

Carl?"

"Oh yeah," Carl said.

"Good. I'm next, then. Okay, boss?"

"Sure, Tony. Might as well get all the use we can out of this sorry piece of shit."

Within a minute, without warning, Carl dumped a salty load of cum in Leo's mouth. Leo had heard that straight guys came quick, but Jesus...

Carl slid off the desk and Tony, cock already out, took his place. Uncut. All three of them uncut. What, in the U.S. of A., were the odds of that?

"Grease him up, Carl. Let's make this a night to remember."

As Leo took Tony's hard-on down his throat, he felt the gun being pulled away, a glob of lube being pushed into his butt, and then the gun again, pushing right in past the tight ring of muscle. "Okay, DeAngelis," Vin Stroker said, "let's see how long this can go on before somebody shoots."

Leo's mind was racing. What was more likely to save his life, holding off Tony's orgasm or doing an extra-fine job in getting him to come? The answer came from Vin, of course. "Get to work, you fuck, if you want to live one minute more." And the gun slid further into his insides.

Leo used every blowjob technique he ever knew, the trick with his tongue, the one with his throat muscles. Unlike Carl, with his scented crotch, Tony tasted like he could use a bath. Funky, but not bad. Like rough trade should taste. He would have sucked this dick even without a gun up his ass.

Vin was pumping the gun barrel in and out of Leo's open butt. This is the way the world ends, this is the way the world ends, Leo thought. He'd been a Lit major. His mom had wanted him to be a teacher. Instead, he was about to be a dead porn casting director.

Tony was pumping his cock up into Leo's mouth now, his thighs tightening. "I'm gonna shoot, boss."

"Now?"

"Now."

"Then I'm gonna shoot, too," Stroker said.

Oh. Jesus, please don't! Please don't! Leo wanted to plead, but his mouth was full.

Tony sprayed his sperm then. And Stroker pulled the trigger. And Leo's ass was filled, not with hot lead, but with lukewarm water.

Laughter. The men were laughing. Even if Leo wasn't really in on the joke, he felt happier than he'd ever felt in his whole life.

"You shoulda seen his face, Vin!" Tony gasped. "Priceless."

The gun pulled out of Leo's butt. "You can stand up now, Mr. Casting Director," Vin chortled. Leo spun around to face Stroker. His grin was no longer evil. It was handsome.

Vin raised the squirtgun to Leo's face and shot a stream of water into Leo's desert-dry, slackjawed mouth.

"Still don't get it, Leo? Carl's my lover, has been for years. And, yeah, Tony is his brother. He's bisexual. And my Dad? He's an accountant in Westwood. The closest he ever got to the mob was watching Susan Lucci in *Mafia Wife*."

"And?" Leo was still missing something.

"So how about it, Mr. Casting Director?" Stroker grinned. "Did I prove I could act?" He kissed Leo on the mouth then. It was most assuredly not the Kiss of Death.

Well, Kris did get the part in *Studmen* as promised. But by the time the shooting started, the guys at Redhot were already creating a star vehicle tailored to Vin Stroker's particular talents; *Gangland Gangbang* turned out be their biggest money-maker yet.

Kris, uneasy with Stroker's ascendant star, took his somewhat tired act to Hotrod Films, where, under Barry Stein's mismanagement, his career went down the toilet. Vin Stroker, on the other hand remains the hottest thing the adult film industry has seen since—well, since porn was shot on actual film stock.

The arson fire at the Redhot offices didn't do any real harm, just some smoke and water damage. Fortunately for the cops, the place was ransacked before it was torched; the perps were apprehended when they tried to use Bryan's stolen American Express card. They turned out to be two pimply teen-aged boys from the Escondido branch of ChristAlmighty, and they ratted on each other really quick.

The strain of the fire was one stress too many for Bryan Ng and what he referred to as his "delicate constitution." He quit at the peak of his video-making career, moved to Amsterdam, and started making a mint running adult websites.

Leo DeAngelis took over the business, made Mike his Casting Director and personal cocksucker, and went on to produce some of the best gay porn ever made. And to this day he keeps his body shaved. He thinks it feels great.

Passport To Porn

David MacMillan

"FIND ME A NEW JOHAN PAULIK OR EMIL KYS," J.R. TOLD ME. "BETTER make it both of them. Global Entertainment needs that kind of appeal to gain more market share."

I didn't like the way he was suddenly looking at me. "You need it to build your name as a director."

"What's wrong with cute American boys?" I asked the man sitting at his desk in the penthouse office overlooking the Pacific Ocean. "There's lots of them all over this country."

The owner of Global Entertainment, glared at me as if I'd just shit on his white, three inch thick carpet.

"Forget them. The market today wants boy-next-door with skin on his wienie." This was from the fifty-year-old man who'd made several small fortunes paying cut American boys to fuck and suck their way through Global's vids.

Who had privately auditioned every guy Global ever put on the payroll like he had me—taking my butch, virgin, just-out-of-film-school-ass in a slam dunk the day he interviewed me.

"You want to become a big director, Jeb, you find yourself someone to direct—more than one of them. Guys with real appeal like those European boys."

He pushed himself out of his overstuffed chair and smiled at me.

"You can do it, Jeb Stuart," he told me as he rounded his desk, his voice almost friendly, like a pit bull slobbering. "Pick up your ticket on your way out. You leave tomorrow." He took my hand in his and shook it.

End of discussion. My employment was on the line, too; that had been J.R.'s implied threat. The two vids I had directed the past year had been near-duds. The two I assisted on the year before were hardly better. The porn industry was changing and I had to change with it, or else.

I had asked for my meeting with J.R. because I could see that my future wasn't in the best of shape. I planned on suggesting that I go into the heartland to find some boy-next-door types for a really nice, down-home-type fuckathon which I would, of course, direct. I never got the chance. Instead of being as corny as Kansas in August, I was being packed up and sent out to the minor leagues. To central Europe.

I gazed out on the old city across the river, one rested boy after sleeping through yesterday afternoon and last night once I got to this armpit of a town. I was in Prague, in the Czech Republic. It had been one long flight and I arrived in the middle of yesterday afternoon— dead-ass tired.

Well, never let it be said that old J.E.B. Stuart's namesake and great-great-great-grandnephew wasn't every bit as ingenious as Robert E. Lee's second in command. Only, this boy wasn't going to get himself killed like the old man did. I was going to be just as ingenious, and avoid the stupidity that got Uncle Jeb ten times removed shot off his horse just before Gettysburg started.

I didn't speak Czech. But, then, J.R. thought everybody in the world spoke English. I knew better. I had the name and phone number of Prague University's gay student league before I left Global Entertainment with ticket in hand to go home and pack.

The first thing I did once I was in my hotel room was call the student league and ask for someone who could speak English. When I had some perky sounding girl on the phone, I told her I needed a gay English-speaker. I explained to her that it didn't matter what sex my homosexual translator was but that he/she would be involved in some pretty deep sexual discussions with gay men. I also told her I'd pay fifty dollars to her organization if they helped me out. She promised to have someone for me the next morning. With that, I fell on the bed and was off to dreamland.

He called me at eight o'clock, just as I was waking up. His voice was young, yet deep. It was also guarded, which I picked up on even through the thick accent. We agreed to meet at ten on the bridge over the Charles River that led from my side of town into the old city. I decided to hoof it—wearing tight black chinos, a muscle shirt, and a jeans jacket. It was more than a little nippy but I was running late getting on with the rest of my life.

Jan Tonkovic was standing in the center of the bridge's walkway as I approached. I saw the sandy—almost ash—blond hair first, worn short but with bangs that reached his eyebrows. As I drew closer, I could make out the angles that contoured his face. Closer still, I saw he was tall, at least six feet, and slim. Long legs too. He was wearing a white long sleeve shirt and loose-fitting cords in early autumn. I figured him to have a swimmer's build.

I knew I wanted to see more of him before I even reached him— preferably with a lot fewer clothes on. The guy was definitely boy-next-door material. He was looking at least as good as the surfer dudes I'd thought were the sum total of my type and I had to admit my tastes were already changing. Maybe J.R. did have it right after all. Thinking about it, I had to admit that he usually did.

"You are Jeb Stuart?" Jan asked as I came to a stop before him.

I grinned and stuck out my hand. "You must be Jan Tonkovic." He studied my hand between us for a long moment before taking it in his, giving it two perfunctory pumps, and letting it go. My cock twitched right on cue: I wanted Mr. Jan Tonkovic.

"We may talk over a coffee, Mr. Stuart?"

"Please, call me Jeb," I told him as I tried to read the guy. "And, yes, I'd like a cup of coffee."

"Will you want good coffee then, or the rubbish we have learned to make for the tourists?"

"Whatever you'd like to drink," I answered and wondered what I was letting myself in for. The way he'd said "tourists," I didn't want him thinking of me as one. Not as much as I wanted in his pants, I didn't.

He led me down cobblestone streets that were narrower than New York City alleyways. Up and down the steep hills of the old city. Between three- and four-storied houses that were older than St. Augustine, Florida. "We go to a student cafe, yes?" he asked over his shoulder. I huffed and puffed, falling further behind him with each hill. I was suddenly realizing all that home Soloflex stuff I had in my apartment back in LA wasn't all that great for getting a guy into real shape.

He finally stopped before a building, looked back at me and laughed. "You Amerikanski are worse than even the Germans," he told me and waved for me to follow him as he dove down the steepest flight of stairs I'd ever seen.

"You'd better damned well be a great fuck," I gasped under my breath as I followed slowly after him into the bowels of the earth.

He hadn't even built up a sweat when I finally reached the bottom of the stairs and found him waiting for me at a door under an old converted gas lamp.

"Are you well, Jeb?" he asked solicitously as I neared him.

"Yeah," I gasped. "Why?" I looked at him sharply but he seemed genuinely concerned.

"You perspire like a man in heat." He smiled and all those bones at all those sharp angles just blended together like angels are supposed to look. "It is less than thirteen degrees."

I started to protest but realized he wasn't talking about lust but the weather, and that he was operating on Celsius and probably meant it was around fifty-five in Fahrenheit. You're gonna find out what kind of shape I'm in, I thought, just as soon as I'm porking you. I decided then I wasn't going to use any lubricant when I was shoving my prong into his ass the first time I got him. He was going to feel each of my eight inches push into his butt—good. He was going to feel me get even. Oh, yeah!

He found us a table—with four other people elbow to elbow with us. I silently fumed. We needed to talk business and here he was putting us down right in the middle of every young person in this damned city. A truly cute (to die for) boy came over and pulled bangs out of his face. There was some discussion and Jan looked over at me. "You are paying in dollars, yes?" I nodded. The discussion continued.

The boytoy left with our order and Jan said: "I have ordered us a good breakfast, Jeb. You will love it—"

I had instant visions of this boy I was lusting for imagining a wallet stretched wide in green paperbacks. "How much?" I demanded.

He studied me, his brows furrowing. "Less than six dollars American—give him four more dollars as gratuity and Jaroslav will suck your dick here at the table."

I gasped and glanced quickly at our companions. They didn't seem to have heard—at least, they were ignoring us.

Jan laughed. "Most Czechs do not speak English, Jeb. For so long, the two foreign languages the Ministry of Education recommended were Russian and German. I spoke all three well enough by my thirteenth year." I tried to imagine fluently speaking three of the hardest languages in the world and couldn't. "Now you will tell me what it is that you wish translated and how much you are willing to pay for the service."

For the next half hour we discussed my job and what I wanted him to do. For the next two hours we haggled about what I would pay. Jan Tonkovic was a young, smart, good-looking guy who had an idea of how much he was worth. I was a few years older and maybe not as smart, but I knew he lived in a backward part of the world and that counted for a lot. We settled on two American dollars an hour, paid daily—and unreported.

"And what does that include?" I asked.

"Being your translator, Jeb," he answered, looking at me in surprise. "While you recruit these men and, later, when you tell them what to do and how to do it."

"I'd like to get to know you better, Jan," I said, putting it out in the open and forgetting the others at our table.

"So that I can become one of your actors, Jeb?" He shook his head, his bangs falling over those grey eyes. "So that all of America can see me naked and making sex with any boy? That is not possible."

"You don't have to be in the movie. I just think you're a nice guy I'd like to get to know better." It was like I was working a straight boy toward my bed and the fun I was going to show him there.

His thin lips twisted slowly into a smile. He looked directly into my eyes as he covered my hand with his. "We shall see, Jeb."

I felt that I could have floated up to the ceiling at that moment if his hand wasn't holding me down. Not one of the thirty or so guys I'd porked over the past few years had gotten to me so fast. I figured Jan was going to be a really special fucktoy the next couple of months. I forgot all about how cute Jaroslav was.

The week that followed was a whirlwind of activity and soon I had ten of the cutest guys in the world signed up and getting me proof of their ages. Jaroslav from the restaurant was the first one I signed. I had photos of them butt-naked, spread-eagled, soft and hard, hairy balls and ass. I even stopped being aware of the skin covering their cockheads by the end of the week. My dick was staying hard by the time I'd signed up the last one. And I had them exclusive, too—if they appeared on anybody's TV screen in the next three years, I was going to get my share. He was going to be pissed, but I'd learned a lot of things from J.R. over the past two years.

I was hornier than a bull with a herd of heifers grazing in front of his pen. I'd been a week with nothing but solo relief. Jaroslav had managed to grope me, the other nine just made it plain one way or the other that they were available. All I needed to do was show interest. Right there in front of Jan Tonkovic.

I hadn't. I couldn't understand myself. I had ten cute boytoys waiting for me to feed them my tool and I was as deep into self-denial as a preacher at his own funeral. Hell! I'd hardly noticed any of those guys while they were in my room strutting their stuff for me. It was only after I wined and dined Jan like a breeder going for the score and he had left for the night that I would look at the day's photos and find out just how interesting they were.

Jan Tonkovic. He was all I could think about.

Him! The son of a bitch was a wooden Indian without the woody.

The guy just smiled at me when I suggested we go out. "I must study some time, Jeb. I study at night."

Yeah! Right! I wanted to study too. Him. His ass. How good it felt gripping my pole. How his lips tasted. How his nips felt on my tongue. How his body felt against mine.

"Jesus!" I growled as I shut the door of my room behind the last cute rump I'd put in my revue and turned back to face Jan. "You don't even get hard looking at all this beefcake, do you?"

"You wish to know if I think of sex, Jeb?" he asked softly, studying me as if he'd never thought of it before.

"Yeah. Didn't you want to get it on with any of the guys we've seen this week? Wouldn't you like to get into a fuck right now? To get your rocks off? You and me? I know I would."

He stared silently at me for a seemingly endless moment. Those grey eyes blinked and a smile formed on his lips, lifting his angled cheeks. "You want to make sex with me, Jeb?"

I grinned, sure of where things were heading now. "That'd sure do for starters." I took a step toward him and tried to imagine how good his ass was going to feel under me.

"Why did you not relieve yourself with them?" Jan nodded toward the door. "Any of them would have been good."

"I don't do three-ways."

"Three-ways?"

"You, me, and whoever. Besides, I want you alone. I've wanted you since I first saw you." I frowned and took another step. "I want more than just a quick fuck, Jan—now. I'd like us to team up while I'm here."

"Team up while you are here." He nodded. "I would be your Czech boyfriend, yes?"

"Yeah," I answered as I reached him. I raised my hand and spread it across his closest pec. My thumb and forefinger closed around his nipple.

He pursed his lips and nodded. "I will accept an American boyfriend to have sex with—while he is here." His hand touched my arm and he smiled. "Unless I find a lover before you leave."

I didn't like the way that sounded but I shrugged it off. I was close to getting what I'd wanted all week. My first piece of Czech ass. Jan's. Yeah.

Both of his hands moved to my back, pulling me to him. Then, our lips were pressed together and his tongue was negotiating with my teeth. I opened up. His hands moved down to grasp my butt and I ground my cheeks against them, caught up in finally having the man I wanted.

His fingers made their way between us, avoiding my hard meat, and deftly opened the button at the waist of my chinos. I threw my arms around his back, pulling us closer. Fingers from both of his hands gripped my waistband at the hips and pulled out, forcing the zipper down as I ground my hard cock against his.

I was past thinking. My balls rode my dick and enough pre-come was flowing through my piss-slit that my underwear was already wet. I couldn't get enough of Jan's mouth. And I wasn't about to break our contact to unbutton his shirt. I pulled it from his trousers as his hands slid beneath my underwear and grabbed my cheeks hard.

He released them a moment later and moved his hands around my hips, forcing my chinos and underwear onto my thighs. "You want me, do you, Jeb?" he asked, breaking our kiss, when he found my boner.

"Yeah. Oh, yeah, I want you," I groaned as one hand dove for the front of his cords. The other hand held the hem of his shirt at his armpits because I was going tit-licking. I couldn't remember ever being as hungry for anybody as I was for Jan Tonkovic at that moment. Shit! He'd had nearly a week to grow on me and he was that fine.

I had his pants down to his knees before my tongue could reach his nipple. I caressed my cheek against his smooth, tight chest as my teeth sought out the rosy nubbin. My hands eased his old-styled boxers over his butt and he gasped as I gently bit down on his tit.

I started down his chest with my lips and tongue, onto his taut belly, moving toward the heat I could feel rising under my chin. My fingers found the tight curls of his pubes as my tongue fucked his belly button. He groaned as my fingers started around the base of his meat. And couldn't find each other.

I halted my downward trek as awareness began to creep over me. I sat back on my haunches to look at him and take stock of his weapon.

The dick that faced me was huge. My fist moved out around the thick shaft, trying to find a place where my fingertips could meet. Stretched skin bunched over his helmet. The thing had to be at least nine inches. Jan Tonkovic was so fucking hung, I didn't know if I could even get past his cockhead to give him a good time before he was giving me one.

"We should get on the bed, perhaps?" Jan asked and I looked up past his belly, up past his muscled chest, into his grey eyes smiling down at me.

"Yeah, maybe we should," I allowed as I found myself swimming in those deep, lovely grey eyes—and forgot everything else.

His hands on my shoulders raised me. His thin lips touched mine as I stood before him. His tongue entered my mouth and we kissed as he guided us to my Holiday Inn double bed. One of his legs settled between mine, spreading them as I sat on the bed and lay back with him following me down, our tongues still dueling.

I tried to roll him over but he stayed on top me, his hand moving down my left thigh to my knee. He raised my leg onto his butt and I knew what he wanted. I gasped, breaking away from his lips.

I stared up into his smiling eyes and was again lost in them. "Do you have those fine American condoms, Jeb?" he asked as he settled between my legs. "Those that are already lubricated?" He sucked his index finger, holding my gaze with his, and brought it down below my balls.

We were at that point. In for a penny, in for the whole enchilada. That's what I'd told every boy I'd plowed and what J.R. told me when I found out he didn't bottom at my job interview. In other words, it was a little late to back out now. His finger pressed against my assmuscle and I pushed down to open it for him. The smile that had been in his eyes spread over his face. Never taking my eyes off him, I reached over and began rummaging in my open suitcase beside us.

I found the large box of rubbers I'd packed back in LA and smiled up at him as I pulled one packet out for us.

"Put it on me, Jeb. I am going to give you sex that you have only dreamt of having."

I tore the foiled packet open faster than I had when I was about to get my first boy. Anticipation sizzled through me like a brushfire as I quickly rolled the latex over Jan's cockhead and onto his shaft. I wanted him in me. I wanted him fucking me. I wanted him to possess me. "Take it slow and easy, lover," I told him, "it's been a while." I raised my legs onto his shoulders as he situated himself.

His lips nibbled my earlobe as I felt him position himself against my back entrance. His tongue traced my jaw as I adjusted to him being there and my ass hiked in the air. His lips crushed mine as he lowered his groin, and his tongue unfurled into my mouth when I opened it to protest.

I saw stars as the Washington Monument began to shove into my asshole. Pain surged out of my guts over my whole body. I whimpered and lost my erection. I tried to tell myself it wouldn't last but my body wasn't believing it. His tongue played tiddlywinks with my tonsils.

My sphincter gave up at that moment and spread wide enough to let a train in. Jan fell into me and was halfway in before he slowed down his steamroller entrance. He broke his possession of my mouth and pushed himself up to look down at me. "Do I hurt you too much, Jeb?"

I saw only concern in his face as he studied me. I smiled back at him weakly. "It only hurts when I laugh," I joked.

His brows furrowed in question and I reached around my legs to grab his asscheeks. I pulled him to me until I felt his pubes tickling the insides of my thighs.

I began to grind against him in me. I felt his balls spreading across the top of my asscheeks and his bush scratching the bottom of my balls. "Get me hard, lover," I told him. "Jack me off while you fuck me." I gave him my best smile of approval when his fingers began to caress my soft meat. "Fuck me good, baby."

I grew quickly under his fingers. He smiled down at me when he could begin to stroke my meat with his fist. "I give you good sex, Jeb?"

I nodded, closed my eyes, and smiled. And gave myself up to our fuck.

My cock was rock hard and my balls rode close to my shaft as Jan's hand stroked it. The rhythm of his strokes into my butt hadn't changed—long, slow, easy movement. He kissed my closed eyes and nibbled at my tits. I was floating toward orgasm, but I knew it wasn't going to be just an explosion of my ball juice. The orgasm waiting for me was one of mind and spirit, as well as body.

I had become Jan Tonkovic's as he first began to fuck me. It was more than just sexual possession. I had wanted him all week long, since I first laid eyes on him—but that desire was deeper than just getting him naked and into bed. I had fallen in love with my translator from Prague University, even if I hadn't known it.

I felt my balls churn. My dick expanded in Jan's fist. I opened my eyes to see him smiling down at me. I was being pulled into the whirlpool that was my orgasm. Jan's cock moved familiarly within by ass, massaging my joyspot with its every stroke. I could barely catch my breath, I was so close.

My balls couldn't hold it any longer and I felt my lava push into my cumchute. My eyes widened and I bucked my hips in reflex to the rush of jizz through my cock.

My assmuscles clamped down on Jan's meat and began to milk it as rope after rope of lava sprayed out of my dick. I heard him gasp and felt him push his cock deep into my ass. I felt his meat expand to stretch my gut tauter. But none of it connected as I continued to shoot my load.

When I finally came down I found Jan lying on top of me, trying to catch his breath as I was mine. "That was good," I mewled contentedly.

"It was better than good, Jeb—and that is a problem," he said and pushed himself up onto his knees, pulling himself from me. "One I feared."

I felt empty with his meat disconnected from my ass and looked up at him curiously. "What's wrong with that, baby?"

"If it is too good, making sex becomes making love."

"We were making love…"

"No. We cannot make love. Making love is for lovers. Making sex is for just friends."

I stared at him, trying to understand him and fighting against feeling like a fucktoy who'd just been fucked. "I want to be lovers."

"We can't be. You make your sex film and you leave for America. I shall still be here. That is okay for casual friends who make sex; it is not okay for lovers who make love."

I understood and smiled. In for a penny, in for the whole enchilada. I hadn't found anybody who made me feel like Jan did. What the fuck? I could stay here and do vids of some of the cutest guys on earth fucking and sucking. J.R. would probably love for me to be half a world away. It didn't matter where I lived as long as I had ashblond, grey-eyed Jan Tonkovic beside me. And in me. I went for a reality check on that one. And knew instantly I meant it. I wanted him fucking me.

"And if I lived here? Would you be my lover then? And make love to me like you just did?"

Tears clouded his eyes as he grabbed me and pulled me to him.

It was five o'clock in the evening in Prague when I picked up the phone and called LA. It was eleven o'clock in the morning in LA when I got J.R. on the line. I gazed at Jan, lying naked across the bed watching me, and smiled as a thought hit me. This bed was my casting couch—it was both of ours. It had brought us together, even over the chasms made by language and culture.

"I have boys—ten of them, J.R.," I told him. "The hottest guys you'll ever see. They're under contract to me." He wasn't happy with that part. I waited until he stopped telling me what I'd done to my mother and what she hadn't done with my father. "I want to make four vids a year with these guys—will you finance and distribute them? And put me on a royalty basis?"

There was more argument from LA but we agreed to meet Tuesday morning so he could look at the photos of the boys. If they were as good as I said they were, I'd have my backing.

I turned to Jan as I hung up the phone. "Do you have your passport?"

"Of course. But why?"

"Monday we fly to LA." I saw his concern and before he could voice it, I said: "I have to move out of my apartment there, put things in storage…" I smiled and took his hand in mine. "I've got to make sure I'm earning a living if I move over here."

He kissed me then. My hand found his rockhard cock. I pushed away and smiled at him. "Come here, let's put this thing on you," I said as I took another condom from my box.

"Tomorrow, we find us a flat, Jeb," he told me as I lay back and put my feet on his shoulders.

About the Authors

BARRY ALEXANDER (Garage Sale) Barry is an Iowa-based freelance writer. His collection of short erotica, *All The Right Places*, was published by Badboy in 1997. His fiction has appeared in a number of gay magazines and in the following anthologies: *Friction* (Alyson, 1998), *Skinflicks* (Companion Press, 1999), *The Young And The Hung* (Prowler,1999), and *Friction 2* (Alyson, 1999)

MURRAY BROWN (Cock Rock) Murray loves the New York Yankees, Impressionist art, and his cat Mike. In addition to working in record sales and promotions, he has been a bartender, a DJ, and an actor. An aspiring writer, this is Murray's first published story.

ALEX COREY (Crashers) Alex works hard to overcome the Puritanical inclinations of his native New England. His fiction and poetry has appeared in several publications, among them *Christopher Street* and *Advocate Classifieds*.

BILL CRIMMIN (Stunt Cock) Bill makes his home in Canvey, in Essex. This is his first published work. Other stories have been accepted for future publication in several anthologies due from *STARbooks*.

GEORGE DIBBS (The Life Saver) George is a self-described beach bum with a strong preference for the Gulf of Mexico. Writing is one of his hobbies but this is his first published work. Some of George's longer works can be found on-line at (http://library.gaycafe.com/nifty/) and (http://www.assgm.com).

VIC HOWELL (In Search Of…) Vic is a well-established Southern writer and Dave MacMillan's partner. Vic's fiction has appeared in several other anthologies, including *Skinflicks* (Companion Press, 1999).

DAVID LOGAN (In Security) David has been writing fiction for the past five years—science fiction, children's fiction and one action-adventure story. This is his first published work. Several of David's longer pieces of fiction can be found on-line at (http:// www.library.gaycafe.com/nifty/)

TOM MACDOUGAL (The Headmaster And The Rent Boys) This is Tom's first published story. He grew up in Glasgow and attended University in Edinburgh, where he met his lovers Karl and Emil—with whom he now lives in Berlin.

DAVID MACMILLAN (Passport To Porn) David is a Brit ex-pat currently living in Georgia. He has been writing for fifteen years and his stories have appeared in most American gay magazines. His stories have also appeared in *Skinflicks* (Companion Press, 1999) and *The Mammoth Book of Historical Erotica* (Robinson, 1998).

ALAN W. MILLS (How To Be A Pornstar) Alan is a California-born Gen-X writer and poet living in West Hollywood, California. He currently serves as the editor of *In Touch, Indulge*, and *Black-male*. He often writes under the names Alain du Moulinet, Dante Williams, and Jeff Kane. His story "Pornstar Powertrip" appeared in the anthology *Skinflicks* (Companion Press, 1999).

BRYAN NAKAI (Dances With Coyote) Bryan is a Native American who lives in Albuquerque, New Mexico. He is currently involved with a computer programmer. Neither of them has ever kidnapped a tourist. This is Bryan's first published story.

J.D. RYAN (Stairway To Stardom) J.D. lives in South Carolina, and has been published in *In Touch* magazine and a number of sci-fi magazines. His website address is http://members.aol.com/ DKSYD/

RUTHLESS (Screen Test) Ruthless has been writing fiction for his own enjoyment for nearly twenty-five years. "Screen Test" is the first story that he has ever submitted for publication. He lives in New Brunswick, Canada. Some of his other work can be found on-line at (http:// www.assgm.com).

DOMINIC SANTI (Special Talent) Dominic is a Los Angeles-based freelancer whose contributions have appeared in the anthologies *Sex Toy Tales* (Down There Press, 1998), *The Erotic Web: Threads From the Internet* (Dreams Unlimited, 1998), *The Mammoth Book Of Historic Erotica* (Robinson, 1998), *Hard At Work* (Masquerade, 1998), *Friction 2* (Alyson, 1999), and *Ravish Me* (Masquerade, 1999). Partnered for many years, Santi shares a home office with a dog and several opinionated cats.

SIMON SHEPPARD (Made Man) Simon's work has been

published in dozens of anthologies, including *Best American Erotica of 1997* (Alyson); the 1996, '97, and '99 editions of Best Gay Erotica (Cleis Press); *Midsummer Night's Dreams* (Masquerade, 1998); *The Mammoth Book of Historical Erotica* (Robinson, 1998); the Lammy Award-winning *Bending The Landscape* (Overlook Press, 1999); *The Ghost of Carmen Miranda* (Alyson, 1998); *Noirotica 3* (Rhinoc Eros, 1998): *Guilty Pleasures* (Masquerade 1999); and *Skinflicks* (Companion Press, 1999). With M. Christian, he is co-editor of *Rough Stuff: Tales Of Gay Men, Sex, and Power* (Alyson, 1999). Some of his stories have also appeared online at (www. fishnet mag.com).

MICHAEL STAMP (Type Casting) Michael's secret forays into the gay male porn industry provided the spark for "Type Casting" and several other tales. He makes his home, discretely, in a small New Jersey suburb.

W.M. WILLIAMS (Nice Work If You Can Get It) Williams makes his professional debut in these pages. No stranger to the keyboard, he has worked as a print and broadcast journalist.

visit the
companion press
gay adult book
website
to view our
complete catalog
book excerpts
author interviews
photos, reviews
news & events
and our
free offer!

other books from **companion press**

SEE ORDER FORM REVERSE SIDE

companion press order form

PO Box 2575, Laguna Hills, CA 92654 USA • Fax Orders (949) 362-4489
Phone Orders 1-800-373-0759 Mon.-Fri. 7 AM - 11 AM Pacific Standard Time

Please include your phone or E-mail (for questions about your order only):

_____

PRINT Name_____

Address _____

City _____ State _____ Zip _____

PLEASE PRINT CLEARLY. USE EXTRA SHEET OF PAPER IF NECESSARY

Qty	ISBN # last 3 digits only	Title	Price (each)	Price

SHIPPING & HANDLING CHARGES
(Sorry, we no longer ship books or videos outside the U.S.)
BOOK Shipping & Handling Charges (U.S. ONLY)
First book $4.00. $1.00 for each additional book.
VIDEO Shipping & Handling Charges (U.S. ONLY)
First Video $5.00. $1.00 for each additional video.
RUSH FedEx Delivery Charges (U.S. ONLY)
Check one and ADD to above charges ❑ Overnight, Add $17.00
❑ 2nd Day, $12.00 ❑ Saturday Delivery, Add $31.00.
CREDIT CARD or MONEY ORDERS ONLY for rush delivery.

Subtotal	$
Discount or Credit (if any)	-
California Residents add 7.75% Sales Tax	$
Shipping & Handling See left for rates	$
ADD RUSH FedEx Delivery Charge	$
TOTAL	$

Check Payment Method
❑ Visa ❑ MasterCard ❑ American Express ❑ Money Order
❑ Check (**Allow 6-8 weeks.**) Make check payable to COMPANION PRESS.

Credit card # _____ Exp. date _____

X Signature required for all orders
_____

I certify by my signature that I am over 21 years old and desire to receive sexually-oriented material. My signature here also authorizes my credit card charge if I am paying for my order by Visa, MasterCard or American Express. We cannot ship your order without your signature.

❑ **Here is my $5 for your complete book and video offers ($5 is refundable with your first purchase). I do not wish to order at this time.**

0599